The Doctor's Apprentice

For Bennett.

Happy reading!

Ann Walsh

Also by Ann Walsh

Flower Power (Orca, 2005)
By the Skin of His Teeth (Dundurn, 2004)
Shabash! (Dundurn, 1994)
The Ghost of Soda Creek (Dundurn, 1990)
Moses, Me and Murder (Pacific Educational, 1988)
Your Time, My Time (Dundurn, 1984)

Edited by Ann Walsh

Dark Times (Ronsdale, 2005)
Beginnings: Stories of Canada's Past (Ronsdale, 2001)
*Winds Through Time: An Anthology of Canadian Historical
Young Adult Fiction* (Dundurn, 1998)

The Doctor's Apprentice

A Barkerville Mystery

Ann Walsh

Ann Walsh

A SANDCASTLE BOOK
A MEMBER OF THE DUNDURN GROUP
TORONTO

First edition 1998
Second edition 2007

Editor: Michael Carroll
Design: Jen Hamilton
Printer: Webcom

Library and Archives Canada Cataloguing in Publication Data

Walsh, Ann, 1942-
    The doctor's apprentice / by Ann Walsh.

ISBN 978-1-55002-633-7

    I. Title.

PS8595.A585D62 2007   jC813'.54   C2007-901097-0

1   2   3   4   5   11   10   09   08   07

We acknowledge the support of the Canada Council for the Arts and the Ontario Arts Council for our publishing program. We also acknowledge the financial support of the Government of Canada through the Book Publishing Industry Development Program and The Association for the Export of Canadian Books, and the Government of Ontario through the Ontario Book Publishers Tax Credit program, and the Ontario Media Development Corporation.

Care has been taken to trace the ownership of copyright material used in this book. The author and the publisher welcome any information enabling them to rectify any references or credit in subsequent editions.

J. Kirk Howard, President

Printed and bound in Canada.
Printed on recycled paper.
www.dundurn.com

Dundurn Press
3 Church Street, Suite 500
Toronto, Ontario, Canada
M5E 1M2

Gazelle Book Services Limited
White Cross Mills
High Town, Lancaster, England
LA1 4XS

Dundurn Press
2250 Military Road
Tonawanda, NY
U.S.A. 14150

*This book is dedicated with much love and many thanks
to Mauri Clemons-Braund, my sister and my friend*

Acknowledgements

I owe many thanks to Dr. Alec Holley of Quesnel for lending me his treasured copy of *The Physician's Vade Mecum*. Thanks also to Dr. Glenn Fedor of Williams Lake and everyone at Kornak and Hamm's Pharmacy for their help with my medical research. I would also like to thank the British Columbia Arts Council for a grant I received during the writing of this book.

One

The heavy trap door of the gallows slammed against its supports, the crowd gasped, a woman cried out.

"It is done," said a man's voice. "He is dead, hanged as sentenced by the judge."

The August heat covered me, thick as a wool blanket, and I felt the sweat on my face as I listened to the sounds of death. The others who had come to watch the hanging had not noticed me sitting under a tree, hidden by its branches. Nor had I been able to *see* what was happening, although I had *heard* everything.

I wanted to go home, but my legs felt too weak to carry me down the road, away from the courthouse and the newly built gallows. I could not stand. I could not move.

From behind me, someone whispered, "Ted."

I jumped, and my heart began to beat rapidly. Who was calling my name? I leaned my face against the pine tree, feeling the roughness of its bark against my cheek, and put both my arms around its trunk. I clung tightly to the tree, refusing to look into the shadows.

"Ted," said the voice once more.

"Who is it?" I asked, my voice so low that I could scarcely hear the words I spoke. "Who is there?"

"A friend," he said with a threatening laugh.

That laugh. I knew it well, knew who it belonged to. Against my will my hands loosened their grip and I felt myself beginning to turn towards the person who had called my name.

A tall man stood there, his hands outstretched in front of him, reaching for me. "Master Percy," he said. "I've a score that I've not yet settled with you." He took a step towards me.

"No," I said. "Leave me alone. Please ..."

The words trailed away and I stood in silence, staring at the tall figure of James Barry, murderer. He took another step and once more I heard the sound of his laughter, a sound I would never forget.

I saw around his neck the thick, tightly knotted rope of the hangman's noose. Then I began to scream.

"Theodore Percival MacIntosh, stop this. Be quiet, son. Wake up."

"Leave him be, Ian. Harsh words will not help to quell his terrors."

My father's voice. My mother's. I was home, in bed.

"You were dreaming, Ted," said my mother, bending over me. "You are clutching your blanket to your face so fiercely you can scarcely breathe. Let it loose, son."

"Ma?" I said.

"Aye, and your father, too," said my Pa. "Now, if you don't mind, I shall go and try to take some rest for what is left of the night. You have a fine voice for singing, son, but I can't say that I care to hear it echoing through the house in the dark."

"Leave the boy alone," said Ma. "The dreams which trouble him cause him far more pain than we suffer as a result of broken sleep."

My father grumbled something and left the room. My mother smoothed the covers around me, tucking them firmly under the mattress.

As she pulled the thick wool blanket from my hands, I realized that in my dream the blanket had become the trunk of the pine tree to which I had clung so tightly. I let go of it reluctantly and Ma finished tidying my bed.

"Your dreams have not let you sleep in peace for many months, Ted. Will you not tell us what terrorizes you so badly that you cry out, night after night?"

I didn't answer. I hadn't talked to my parents about my nightmares, not ever. They had begun in October 1866, shortly after I had gone with Constable Sullivan to arrest James Barry at the suspension bridge in Alexandra. The body of a man had been found, and James Barry, suspected of the murder, was trying to escape from Barkerville, the goldfields and also from my friend Moses, who had evidence that Mr. Barry was guilty of murder.

Moses was supposed to go with Constable Sullivan and help capture Barry, but Moses had fallen ill and I had been sent in his place. Moses and I both knew only too well what James Barry looked like, but the constable had never seen his face; he relied on me to make the identification.

I *had* identified James Barry. He had changed his appearance, but I knew him in spite of his attempts at disguise. I had recognized his laugh, that same laugh which had so recently echoed through my dreams.

It was then, shortly after his arrest, that James Barry had said he had "a score to settle" with me. It was then that the dreams had begun.

Now it was April 1868, eight months after James Barry had been sentenced, tried and hanged, a full year and a half since Constable Sullivan and I had captured him at the Alexandra Bridge. I would be fourteen soon, and was already of a grown man's size. Yet, I was still having childish nightmares.

"I am sorry if I woke you and Pa," I said to my mother.

She stopped fussing with the blanket and looked at me. "You did not answer me, Theodore. Tell me about these dreams which haunt you so."

"I can't, Ma," I said, not meeting her eyes. "I can't."

Even though I suspected that my parents knew full well of what and whom I dreamed, I would never tell them exactly what terrors made me cry out in my sleep. Perhaps I believed that if I didn't speak of them, the nightmares would leave and I, and my parents, could rest undisturbed once more.

I was no longer the cowering twelve-year-old who had been terrified by the bearded stranger who had walked into Moses's barbershop one day and had so changed my life. I wasn't a child anymore. Childish dreams and night terrors should no longer be a part of my life. The dreams must stop, I thought. They must stop.

"The dreams must stop," said my father, echoing my thoughts. "I find it hard to tend to my work when I have had my sleep disturbed. Carpentry is a difficult trade, and when I am tired I make mistakes, costly mistakes."

Ma and Pa hadn't gone back to bed. Their voices were coming from the kitchen and, since Ma had neglected to close my bedroom door, I could hear their conversation clearly.

"You are too harsh on the lad, Ian," said my mother. I heard her drop fresh kindling into the cook stove and stir up the coals to start the fire. "He is young, and he has seen and heard some frightening things. Give him time to recover from them."

"Time?" asked my father. "Night after night, for more than a year, these dreams have torn our sleep to shreds. It has been time enough."

"A while longer, and it will pass. I feel sure of it. Give him just a bit more time."

"Aye, Jeannie, and while he dreams and screams, my time is wasted, as I bungle simple tasks for lack of sleep."

"He is but a child ..." began my mother.

"He is no longer a child," said my father. I heard the heavy iron kettle clang against the stove as he moved it to catch the heat. "He will be fourteen soon, but you treat him as if he were still an infant. Most lads his age have found work in the mines of the goldfields, difficult work. Ted is not a child, Jeannie. You should not treat him so."

"I treat him with love," said my mother. "He may be near-grown, but he will always be my child."

"You coddle him," said my father. "Just now you soothed him as if he were an ..."

"An infant," said my mother. Her voice was high-pitched now, the way it gets when she is upset or angry.

"I heard you when you first said it. I disagree. I do not treat Theodore as if he were still a baby."

There was silence for a while. I wondered if I could get out of bed and close my door quietly enough so that my parents wouldn't hear me. Through a gap in the curtains I could see the pale grey of dawn, and realized that Ma and Pa had decided to make an early start on the day. They would not be returning to sleep.

My parents seldom argued, and I had never heard them speak so sharply to each other. I pulled the blankets over my head, hoping to block out their words.

"There must be some way to help him," said my father. His voice was softer now, less angry. "It hurts me to see the lad so troubled. He comes with me to the carpentry shop, day after day, and he does nothing but make mistakes. Even the simplest chore seems beyond him. Just yesterday he allowed a pot of glue to boil over on the stove while he stood staring at it. His work is useless."

"His heart is not in anything," said my mother. She sighed. "Mr. Malanion, Ted's music teacher, called on me last week. He says that he sees little sense in Ted continuing with his violin lessons. Although Ted tries to practise—I hear him do so—his fingers no longer do as he bids them. The music is gone from his soul, Mr. Malanion says."

I heard a chair being pushed back as my father stood up. Ma was crying and Pa had gone to comfort her. "What shall we do?" I heard her ask.

My father didn't answer for a while and, except for the muffled sounds of my mother's sobs and the low whistle of the kettle, the house was silent.

"I think it is time we sought help outside our family," my father said at last. "It is clear that neither of us can ease Ted's mind and relieve him of the dreams which haunt him. We will ask another for help."

"Who?" asked Ma.

"I don't know," replied Pa. "Let me think on it. But no matter what, those dreams must stop. And soon."

Lying in bed with the covers tight over my head, I did fall asleep, even though I hadn't thought I would. When I awoke for the second time, the streak of grey dawn which made its way through the curtains had brightened into full daylight.

"I have overslept," was my first thought. "Pa will be angry that I am late." For many months now I had been putting in a full day with my father at his carpentry shop, learning the trade which he knew so well. Once he had said that I had the hands of a craftsman and would become a talented carpenter. But then I remembered that earlier this morning he had told Ma that my work was "useless."

Pa was right. I knew that neither my mind nor my heart were in these tasks. But I wanted to be with him. I could try harder, try to still my mind and concentrate on the job at hand. If only I weren't so tired, I thought. If only I could sleep and not dream.

I dressed and went to the kitchen for hot water. Ma was kneading bread, her arms streaked with flour, a frown on her face as she pressed and twisted the dough. She heard me come in, but didn't look up. "You slept late, son. I hope you feel rested."

My mother looked anything but rested. She had dark circles under her eyes, and her face had an unhealthy pallor. I went to her and put a hand on her shoulder.

"I am so sorry that I woke you and Pa again," I said.

"It is not important, Ted."

"Where is Pa?" I asked, changing the subject.

Ma wearily brushed a hand across her forehead, leaving a streak of white flour. "He has gone to the shop, to work."

"Without waiting for me?"

My mother sighed. She still did not meet my eyes.

"Your father thinks that perhaps it is best if you stay home for a few days. He feels you are too tired to be of much help to him."

So that was why Pa hadn't wakened me. I must have fallen asleep before my parents made this decision. My throat was suddenly tight.

Ma went back to her kneading, and I took the kettle from the stove. I returned to my room and washed, then left the house quietly by the front door, without breakfast, without saying goodbye.

Our house is on the road between Barkerville and Richfield, somewhat removed from the noise and bustle of both towns. In Barkerville there are twelve saloons, ten stores, as well as hotels, breweries, restaurants, shoemakers, blacksmiths, barbers and all the other establishments you might expect to find in a busy and prosperous town.

Word of the rich gold strikes to be found in the area had brought people from all over the world into the goldfields. More than ten thousand inhabitants now lived in the towns of Richfield, Marysville, Barkerville and Camerontown along Williams Creek. Barkerville had become a *very* busy and prosperous town.

The road between Richfield and Barkerville, which had been a quiet place to live when we first moved here, was now

crowded with homes and cabins and was not nearly as isolat-
ed as it had once been. But from our home, even over the
sounds of the rocker boxes, winches, the stage rattling by several times a day and the shouts and yells of those working
their claims, I could still hear the bubbling of the creek. I
always found that sound comforting, especially at night, and
I missed it in the winter when the creek froze solid.

The stores and homes of Chinese people filled the upper
end of the town, so Barkerville's Chinatown was the first area
I walked through on my way to Pa's shop. The buildings here
were cramped together, even more closely than they were in
Barkerville's Lower Town.

There were several stores which were full of bins and
shelves of dried herbs and other mysterious things, some rec-
ognizable, some so dry and brittle that I couldn't tell if they
were animal parts or bits of roots and tubers.

One of those stores is owned by Sing Kee. He is an herbalist,
and he sells medicines which are bought not only by the
members of the Chinese community, but also by others in
Barkerville. I had been in Sing Kee's store many times, wondering at the goods which were for sale, and listening to him
as he tried to explain to me which ailments each product
cured. Some people say that Sing Kee's medicines are the
best in the goldfields, even better than those doctors offered.

Many of the Chinese miners had left their families behind
when they came to the land of the "Gold Mountain," which
Pa said was the English translation of the Chinese name for
North America. There were "mountains of gold" here in the
goldfields, underground mountains, and rivers too, of gold.
But you had to stake your claim on the right spot and dig

deeply enough to find them. Some miners, like Billy Barker, the man for whom the town was named, found rich veins of gold, but others laboured for months, even years, digging deep shafts but never uncovering the blue clay, below which the gold was often hidden. Both before and after Billy Barker's famous strike in 1862, there had been miners who found nothing but heartbreak and despair.

I walked by the Chinese Temple, the Tong building. Here the Chinese miners gathered for worship, for meetings, for companionship. They also played games, one called *mah-jong*, another called *fan-tan*. My father said that the Chinese gambled on those games and that a great amount of money had been won and lost in the Tong, enough money to build a whole new town. It was the "White Dove," Pa told me, that people gambled on the most, a game where each day numbers printed on small white tiles were picked, and the people who had bet on those numbers won a lot of money.

Perhaps the reason that the Chinese men spent so much time in the Tong building was that they had nowhere else to go. There were very few Chinese women or children in the goldfields. It was expensive to travel here and many men came alone, waiting for the day they would find their fortune and could afford to send for their families. Pa said that most who had made the long trip from China never saw their wives or children again, but were buried here, in the land of the Gold Mountain. I didn't know if it was true or not, but I had heard that years after a Chinese man had been buried, his bones were dug up and sent home to China, to be buried again in his own country with the bones of his ancestors. I'd never seen anyone digging up a grave in the Chinese cemetery at

Richfield, because I never went near that graveyard; James Barry was buried there.

The Chinese funeral processions went right past our house, and everyone carried food to leave at the grave. I didn't know if the food was for the spirits, or for the dead man to take into the other world with him, in case he got hungry. My friend Moses told me that sometimes miners down on their luck would go to the Chinese graveyard after a funeral and steal the food. I had never tasted any Chinese food, but I thought that a person would have to be extremely hungry to eat a meal served beside a newly dug grave. Then, just as I was thinking about graves and death, I passed by a building behind the Tong.

It was only a cabin, smaller than most of those in Barkerville, with only one tiny window and a narrow door. But this cabin was where Chinese miners went when they were very old or very sick. Here, lonely men, whose families were far away and could not look after them, went to die. Others brought them food and medicine, cared for them and made them comfortable during their last days and hours. The Chinese had a name for that cabin in their own language, Tai Ping Fong, which meant the Peace Room or the Peace House. To me it was the Death House. I looked away as I passed and walked faster.

The buildings in the lower end of Barkerville were raised on posts so that when Williams Creek was diverted, either by accident or to create a water supply for a claim so that gold could be washed from the gravel, the water stayed away from the houses and stores. Sometimes these diversions caused the creek to burst its banks and come rushing merrily down Barkerville's streets, flooding homes and stores whose foundations were too close to ground level. Even though snow still lay deep on the hills and in the shadows of the buildings, Barkerville's main road was thick in mud today which meant that Williams Creek had thawed and left its normal course once again.

Raising the buildings worked well, except for the fact that no two stores or homes were built at exactly the same height. Boardwalks were erected along the fronts of buildings, but walking along these boardwalks, while it kept your feet out of the mud, meant continually climbing from one level to another and back down again as the walkways followed the different heights of the buildings.

As I passed Moses's barbershop, I realized I hadn't seen him for a while. I stuck my head in the door and he turned to me and smiled.

"Ted. Come in, come in. Sit a spell. I've no customers at the moment so it's a good time for a visit."

"Just for a short while," I said. "How are you, Moses?"

"I am well, if not yet wealthy," laughed Moses. "And you, young man, have grown again."

"Not really, Moses. It's just that you haven't seen me for some weeks."

"I noticed," said Moses. "Now that you spend so much time working with your father I see little of you."

"I'm sorry. I've been busy."

"Busy? Yes. But perhaps maybe you would also prefer to seek other friends, friends more your own age instead of someone of my advanced years."

"You're not old, Moses," I said.

"Not in spirit, perhaps. But the years add up, and they

seem to accumulate much faster once you pass the half-century mark."

Neither one of us spoke for a while, and the silence felt awkward. "I guess I'd better be going," I said. "I'm already late. Pa went without me this morning."

"I know," said Moses. "Your father dropped by here, just after I opened up. He told me that you had a difficult night."

"It was just a dream, that's all."

Moses looked at me for a while before he spoke. "It is not good for you, Ted, to dwell on what has passed."

"I don't 'dwell,'" I said. "I never think about him."

Moses didn't ask who I meant by 'him.' He knew.

"Just now you turned to look all around you," he said.

"As if you suspected James Barry to be lurking in my barbershop. I think he is with you more than you will admit. Perhaps that is why you no longer seek my friendship—because I remind you of a time you would sooner forget."

"That's not true," I said, getting angry. "I wasn't looking for Mr. Barry, I was merely glancing around. He was only in your barbershop twice when I was present, so why would I look for him here?"

"You speak as if he still lives," said Moses. "You carry him with you, in your heart, in your mind, as if he were still alive. That is not healthy."

"It's none of your concern," I said. "I don't care what you believe is healthy. I don't think of James Barry and I don't dream about him."

"I did not speak of dreams, Ted."

"Well, I *don't* dream about him. Ever."

For the second time that morning I left someone without

saying goodbye. I almost slammed the door of the barber-shop on my way out, and I didn't look back at Moses. "I *don't* dream of James Barry," I had said.

How I wished that were the truth.

Two

I didn't look back as I left. Moses had once been my closest friend and I had spent a lot of time sitting on a bench in the corner of his barbershop, listening to the chatter of his customers. But I no longer felt comfortable when I was with him.

Perhaps Moses spoke the truth and it was time I found friends my own age. But where? There were so few young people in Barkerville that the town did not even have a school. Not many women came to the goldfields; there were only a handful of families with babies or small children living here. The goldfields were mainly inhabited by single men, miners who hoped to strike it rich.

My father was right. Most young men of my age in Barkerville would be working. They would have no time for me.

It was warm inside Pa's shop, the small stove burning cheerfully, the smell of wood, shellac, and glue made stronger by the heat in the room. I took off my jacket and hung it up, then pulled on a long leather apron to protect my clothes. My father heard me come in and he lifted his head from his work and looked at me.

"Did your mother not tell you that there was no need for

you to come to the shop today?" he asked.

I nodded, but didn't answer.

"Aye. I see. Well, perhaps it is best that you are here. Take off the apron, there is nothing I want you to do. But there *is* someone I want you to meet."

"Who?" I asked, looking around.

"I believe your father is referring to me," came a voice from behind me. I jumped, startled, and turned around as a tall, slender man came through the door. "You must be Theodore," he said.

"Ted. People call me Ted."

"I am Doctor J.B. Wilkinson," he said, offering me his hand. "Most people call me 'Doc,' but to my friends I am Doctor John or John or simply J.B. You may call me whatever you wish, as long as you do not call me late for supper."

Pa looked confused, but I smiled. "J.B.?" I asked. "A name that is only letters? I would guess that the 'J' stands for 'John,' but what is your middle name?"

"That is a secret I shall carry with me to the grave," answered the doctor. "Only my parents know. No one in Barkerville has ever heard my middle moniker, and even if they knew what it was, no one would dare to call me by it!"

My father laughed. "I believe Ted understands those sentiments only too well, Doctor. He also has an intense dislike of his middle name. We christened him 'Percival' after his great-grandfather, but those who call him that, or the short form, 'Percy,' find out that he also inherited his great-grandfather's temper."

"Pa!" I said. "Please."

"Let me assure you, Ted, that 'Percy' is far better than my

middle name," said Doctor Wilkinson. "But with no disrespect to your ancestor, I find that 'Percy' does not sit well on my lips. I promise I shall never address you that way."

"Thank you," I said, and I meant it. No one used my middle name, no one. Except James Barry. Even in my dreams he called me 'Master Percy,' the way he had when he was alive.

"Percival is a fine name, one which has been in my family for generations," said my father. "I have never understood why the boy dislikes it so." He took a deep breath, and turned to me. "It is good that you came to town today, Ted. It will save Doctor Wilkinson a trip to our home."

"Why is he going to our house? Is Ma ill?"

"No, son, but perhaps *you* are. Go with the doctor so he can examine you. I have told him about your dreams. Now you must speak to him freely."

"I do not need to be seen by a doctor," I said. " I am not sick. Pa, you know that I am healthy and strong and growing taller. You and Ma say that I seem to grow every day. How can I be ill?"

"Ted, your dreams bespeak an illness. If it is not in your body, then the sickness must be in your mind. Perhaps Doctor Wilkinson can be of some help. I want you to go with him and allow him to examine you. At your age a loss of sleep affects you only slightly. Your mother and I, however, can no longer continue suffering because of your dreams. Go with the doctor, Ted."

It was a long speech for my Pa, who usually didn't say much, but this time he could talk for hours and it wouldn't change my mind.

"I am not ill," I said again, "and I have no wish to be seen by a doctor. I will not ..."

Doctor Wilkinson interrupted. "If you feel uncomfortable about coming to my surgery, Ted, perhaps you will accompany me to Wake Up Jake's instead. I had breakfast very early this morning, and I could do with some nourishment about now."

"But, Pa ..." I said, ignoring the doctor.

"Go, son," said my father, and he bent over his work and would not look at me. "Go," he said again.

The doctor touched my shoulder gently. "Ted, I assure you I do not bite my patients, at least not very often. Come with me, but come as a friend rather than as a patient. Patients I have aplenty, but my friends are few. I would welcome your company. We will take an oath never to speak our middle names aloud; we will talk, we will eat and perhaps you will tell me about your nightmares."

"A friend," I thought. Perhaps this doctor with the middle name no one knew *could* be my friend. Also, I was very hungry.

Making a decision, I pulled the leather apron over my head and put my jacket on again. Turning my back on Pa, who still would not look at me, I left the carpentry shop, for the third time that morning ignoring my manners and not saying goodbye.

Doctor Wilkinson put his hand on my shoulder again as we walked. "Don't be angry with your father, Ted. He came to see me early today. He is very concerned about you. I had gone to his shop to inform him that I was on my way to your home to visit you."

"I'm not sick, and I don't think my Pa had any business talking to you about me. Do I *look* ill?"

The doctor laughed. "No, you do not, Ted. You look as healthy as a boy your age should. Yet the health of the mind can not be determined so easily."

"There is nothing wrong with my mind," I said. "I can read and write as well as any man in Barkerville, better than most. My mind is sound."

"And my stomach is empty," said the doctor, pushing open the big double doors to Wake Up Jake's restaurant. "So I suggest we deal first with my stomach and worry about your mind later. Let's eat!"

◔◔

Wake Up Jake's smelled of bread baking, of meat being roasted and of freshly ground coffee. Doctor Wilkinson sat down with a contented sigh and ordered beans and extra sourdough bread without looking at a menu. He asked me what I wanted, but I didn't know what to say. I'd never eaten a meal in a restaurant. The doctor must have sensed that I was unsure, because he smiled and said to the waiter, "Ted will have the same. He looks as hungry as I feel."

"I am," I said. "I've had no breakfast."

"Then this can be both breakfast and your midday meal," he said. "Eat up. Doctor's orders."

The meal was served with hot coffee, fresh bread, and thick preserves. The preserves weren't as good as those Ma makes out of the wild strawberries around our place, but I was too hungry to care. I ate four slices of bread, emptied the jar of preserves and also polished off the bowl of beans.

Neither one of us said much while we ate, but when we

finished, Doctor Wilkinson leaned back in his chair and looked at me. "Well?" he asked.

I pretended I didn't know what he meant. "Yes, thank you, sir. I enjoyed the meal, very much."

He grinned at me. "Please do not call me 'sir.' I much prefer to be addressed as 'J.B.' Try it."

I didn't answer him for a while. I was not at all sure that I wished to call this tall doctor by the same initials as James Barry's.

"I will try." I said at last. "I will try, J.B."

"That was not so difficult, was it?"

"No. But I once knew someone else with those initials, and I ..."

"Ah. The infamous James Barry. Yes, I remember."

"You know what happened?"

"I do, but let me refresh my memory. As I recall, you and Moses recognized an unusually shaped gold nugget stickpin. You suspected that the nugget had been stolen, because it was being worn by Mr. Barry, although Moses knew that it belonged to another man, Charles Blessing. How am I doing?"

"Your facts are correct," I said. "So far."

"When Mr. Blessing was discovered with a bullet hole in his skull, Mr. Barry departed the goldfields in great haste, leaving you hog-tied in a deserted cabin so you couldn't warn the constables of his departure."

I nodded. "Yes, that is what happened."

Doctor Wilkinson looked hard at me before he continued. "A nasty experience for anyone," he said. "You were also the person who identified Mr. Barry at the Alexandra Bridge. You were responsible for his arrest—I remember that well."

I nodded again.

"Now," continued the doctor, "James Barry was tried, sentenced, and hanged. He's dead, been dead since August and it is now late in the month of April. Yet when I mention his name, your face pales and your eyes grow fearful. It is not too hard for me to venture a diagnosis. You dream of James Barry, do you not?"

"I should be going now," I said, and stood up.

"Ted, sit down. Look at me. It is no crime to have nightmares, no failing to be afraid or to have those fears present themselves as dreams. But when you do not speak of your terrors, not even to your parents, then you give those fears great power over you. You were a young boy when you faced Mr. Barry. It is understandable that he would terrify you."

"He does not terrify me," I said.

"Is that the truth, Ted?"

"Yes. No."

"Well? Which is it? Yes or no?"

I took a deep breath and the words seemed to tumble out of me. "In the daylight, I don't think about him, at least I try not to. But when it is dark ... the dreams won't end. Night after night I close my eyes and know that it will be the same, that he will be there, waiting to settle his score with me. Sometimes I scream in the nightmare, sometimes I cry. I tremble and sweat with fear and then I can not sleep easily for the rest of the night. I can not end the dreams no matter how I try. They will not stop!"

"They *will* stop," said the doctor. "I promise you. We will talk more about them, and drag them out of the dark of your sleep and into the bright sunlight so that they will wither and blow away in the wind and never trouble you again."

"Will they? How can you be so sure? How can you promise me that?"

"Because I am a doctor, Ted! We men of medicine know these things." He leaned back in his chair and hooked his thumbs through the suspenders he wore over his rough woollen shirt. The chair slipped and he teetered for a moment before regaining his balance and his dignity. His heavy work boots thumped on the floor as the chair righted itself and J.B. returned to a secure sitting position.

"You don't look much like a doctor," I said, trying not to smile. "You don't seem old enough, and you dress more like a miner than a professional man."

"Ah, you have stumbled onto my secret." He cautiously leaned back in his chair once more, and tucked his thumbs through his suspenders again. "Truth is, I came to Barkerville to be a miner, giving up my years of medical training to follow the lure of gold. But I never did find the Mother Lode, not even a sizable nugget or enough gold dust to flour a bread pan. I did find, though, that Williams Creek, while well supplied with miners and those who would be miners, and those who had been miners, was poorly supplied with doctors. So I sold my claim and returned to my profession."

"But not to your professional wardrobe," I said.

"No, I find these clothes comfortable. They suit me, to indulge in a slight pun. I have no wish to wear the more formal attire of my colleagues."

He stood up, reaching across the table to shake my hand. "We have made a good start, Ted, even though you proved very clever at changing the subject. However I must return to my surgery. I have patients who will, no doubt, be restless at my absence. We will talk again, we will talk a great deal. I, at any rate, will talk a great deal for I always do, and you will, perhaps, find it easier to speak to me now that you have made my acquaintance. But for tonight I will prescribe for you some medication which will assure you a dreamless sleep. Come with me and I will get it before I deal with my patient patients."

"Perhaps they are impatient patients by now," I said.

He laughed. "I like your wit, Ted. Now, to my dispensary where I shall dispense something to dispel your fears, dispose of your dreams and end your distress."

What Doctor Wilkinson gave me was a small green bottle, tightly corked. I held it in my hand as I walked home, once in a while lifting it up to the sunlight filtering through the trees on either side of the road. The liquid inside glistened when the light struck it, and the bottle glowed like a jewel.

This road between Barkerville and Richfield was so familiar to me that I knew every wagon rut and every tree along the way. Here was the snag which fell last winter, blocking the road for a day. Here was the curve where the stage overturned during one rainy spring, and here, just ahead, was the tree where, half-hidden in the branches, James Barry had called out to me and I had first heard his laughter. No matter how many times I walked this road, I could never pass that tree without feeling my heart beginning to race.

But today was different. I deliberately slowed my steps as I drew nearer to the place, not speeding up to pass it quickly, the way I usually did. I had been afraid of him, of James Barry, from the moment I first saw him on this road. I had been frightened of him even before I learned, months later, that I had good reason to be afraid. But no more, no more.

I raised the small green bottle in my hand, held it above my head the way a soldier going into war would flourish his sword.

"Never again," I shouted. "You are banished from my life and from my dreams, Mr. Barry. Can you hear me, Mr. James Barry? You will never frighten me again. Never!"

Three

My mother was leaving our house when I arrived home. She was wearing her bonnet and shawl, and she carried a basket, the one she takes to town when she shops.

"Where were you, Ted?" she asked. "You left without my knowledge, and when I needed more wood for the cook stove I had to fetch it myself as you were nowhere to be found."

"I'm sorry, Ma. I went to the shop."

"Your father sent you home again, I see. Which is just as well as I need the wood box filled. Since you will not be working with your father for the next while, I am counting on having a good supply of firewood split and stacked."

"Yes, Ma."

"You look more like yourself, Ted. Your trip to town has refreshed you. Perhaps it will do the same for me."

"Shall I come with you to carry your purchases?"

"No, I can manage. Just tend to our wood supply. It still is cold at night, and we are running low." As she moved past me she noticed the green bottle in my hand. "What have you there?" she asked.

"Medication," I said. "Pa asked Doctor Wilkinson to see me,

and he prescribed something to help me sleep tonight."

"Let me see," she said, taking the bottle from my hand and uncorking it. She sniffed the contents. "Laudanum," she said. "I know the odour well. My mother used this whenever she had one of her bad spells, and she claimed it gave her much relief. But I have never known it to be prescribed for someone your age."

"J.B. said it would help," I said defensively. "He promised."

"Who is this 'J.B.' and what does he know about laudanum?"

"Doctor Wilkinson," I said. "He asked me to call him J.B. We are friends."

My mother smiled. "I am glad of that, Ted. Although Doctor Wilkinson is a busy man, I am sure he will make time for you if he already thinks of you as his friend."

"He does," I said, as I watched Ma disappear down the road, retracing the route I had just taken. I began to whistle as I set off in search of the axe, almost looking forward to my afternoon's work.

When my mother returned, Pa was with her and carried her basket. I was surprised to see them both, but then realized that it was late and my father's workday had ended. I put down the axe, deciding that I, too, had done enough. I had worked all afternoon, and the stack of freshly split firewood had grown to a substantial size. With the April sun warm on my back, I had not realized how quickly time was passing.

It had been good to be outside, working in the fresh air. Here in the goldfields the winter comes early and stays late, and although spring was a month away, the afternoon's heat promised warmer times soon to come. But tonight the temperature would drop well below freezing, so I would fetch Ma

34

an extra bucket of water in case there was a skim of ice on the creek in the morning.

We ate our evening meal amid laughter. I told my parents about J.B. "Dispense, dispel, dispose, and another word beginning with 'dis.' He crammed all those words into one sentence!"

"He's a clever man," said my father. "Although I confess that sometimes both his wit and his behaviour are difficult for me to understand."

Ma was silent for a moment, then she spoke as if she were answering a question my father had not asked. "Doctor Wilkinson's troubles are over, Ian. I feel sure of that."

"What troubles?"

My parents exchanged glances, looking at each other over my head as if I weren't even in the room. Neither one of them answered me.

"What are you talking about?" I asked.

"Things which are past," said my father, after a long silence. "Difficult times which are best forgotten."

"What difficult times?"

My mother smiled at me. "My curious son," she said. "You have always sought to discover what others wished to keep secret. I am glad you enjoyed Doctor Wilkinson's company. He is a good man."

"Like me, he dislikes his middle name," I said. "He wouldn't say what it is, although it begins with the letter 'B.' Do you know it?"

Pa laughed. "I do *not* know the doctor's middle name. Besides, it is none of your business, Ted. But I *do* know that if you could fetch your fiddle and play us a tune, it would help my dinner settle."

My fingers surprised me with their speed and skill and I played for an hour, wondering why lately I had found it such a burden to practise. I would show Mr. Malanion that I was not ready to abandon my music lessons, and I would go to the carpentry shop and show my Pa that my work was not useless.

When I at last put my fiddle away, Pa had already retired for the night. Ma stoked the fire, setting the kettle near the back and turning down the damper in the stovepipe.

"Good night, Ma. I know we shall all sleep well."

"Good night, son," she said, and handed me the small green bottle J.B. had given me. "There is no dosage written for this. Did the doctor tell you how much you should take?"

"He said to use it just before I went to bed. He said it would help stop the dreams."

"But how much are you to take?"

I thought hard. This morning seemed such a long time ago, and I had trouble remembering exactly what J.B. had said. "Two. Two spoonfuls. Yes, I am sure it was two."

My mother sighed. "Tablespoons or teaspoons, Ted?"

"Is there a difference? Does it matter?"

"A tablespoon is much bigger."

"Tablespoons? Yes, I'm sure that's what he said. Take two tablespoons on retiring."

Ma passed me a spoon and a cup of water. "That's more than my mother's dose," she said, "but perhaps this is a less potent mixture. Here, have some water. The taste may not be to your liking."

It wasn't, but I gulped down the medicine anyway, then hastily swallowed the water. Ma gave me a hug and left the room. I picked up the small lantern to take to my bedroom, but at the door of the kitchen I stopped.

Two spoonfuls? Or was it *three*? Three? Yes, now I was sure that I remembered correctly. I was supposed to take three spoonfuls of the medicine, not two.

I uncorked the bottle once more, and decided not to bother with a spoon. One gulp, that should be about equal to a spoonful, I thought. I took a large swallow and began to re-cork the bottle. Only a small amount of liquid remained and I looked at it, wondering. What exactly *had* J.B. said? Wasn't it "for tonight I shall give you something for a dreamless sleep"? Did that mean I was to take the whole bottle of med-icine tonight? Well, it was a small bottle and there was very little left in it.

"For tonight," the doctor had said. Never mind about tea-spoons and tablespoons and how many. J.B. had meant that I was to use it all in one night. I was sure of that now.

I tilted the bottle to my lips, drained it, picked up the lantern, and went to bed.

The light through my curtains was grey when I awoke and my mother and father were beside my bed. So was Doctor Wilkinson.

"You were right, J.B.," I said, my voice dry and brittle. I swallowed hard, wondering why my mouth was so parched, and spoke again. But my voice was weak, hardly loud enough to reach past my own ears.

"You were right," I said again, louder this time. "I didn't dream."

"Don't try to talk," said the doctor. "Here, drink this. Small sips, now. And again." He held a glass of water to my lips and I drank slowly.

"Thank you," I said, and lay back down. "I am still tired and my head hurts. I think I shall sleep some more."

J.B. shook his head. "You shall do no such thing, young man. Since you've finally opened your eyes, we shall force you to stay awake long enough for me to examine you."

"Not now," I said. "In a while. I'm tired."

"Ted?" My mother was holding my hand so tightly it hurt. "Ted, speak to me."

"Not just yet, Ma," I said. "Let me sleep some more, then I will speak to you. Not now." My eyes closed again.

"None of that, Ted. Up, lad, get up. Mrs. MacIntosh, fetch him a large mug of strong coffee while his father and I get him to his feet. He must start moving to make the drug dissipate, help it clear from his body."

I heard my mother leave the room, then Pa and J.B. each took one of my arms and half pulled me out of bed. "Stand up, Ted," said the doctor. "Make your body move. Come now. Walk."

"I can't," I said, surprised. "The floor will not stay still."

"It is the effects of the laudanum," said the doctor. "The sensation will wear off shortly. Take a step. Good. Now another one."

"I can not," I said again. "Hold me, Pa. The floor moves under my feet. I'm falling."

"I have you son. You'll not fall."

The two of them made me walk around and around my bedroom until Ma came back with a steaming mug of hot coffee.

"Now we are going to sit you on your bed," said the doctor. "You may sit, but you may not lie down. Sip the coffee slowly, but drink it all. Then we shall walk some more."

"I don't want to walk," I said. "I don't want to drink coffee. I'm tired. Why are you making me get up? Look out the window. See, the light is grey, the sun hasn't risen yet. It's too early. Go away and let me sleep."

My father laughed. "Morning was many hours ago, son. The grey light you see is the light of dusk, not dawn. You have slept the day away."

I gulped, swallowing a mouthful of coffee. "It isn't morning?" I asked, and finally began to wonder what everyone was doing in my bedroom, waking me up and making me walk around and drink coffee.

"No, Ted. Morning is long passed."

I thought for a moment. "I guess it was teaspoons. Not tablespoons."

"Most definitely not," said J.B. " I was neglectful in not writing out the exact dosage. That vial contained three night's supply, but you downed it all at once. I can only say that I am glad you have returned to the land of the living, my friend. You were lucky."

My head began to hurt again, the blood pounding in my temples, the pain as sharp as if someone were hitting me on the head with an iron kettle.

"I took it all," I said and, in spite of their efforts to make me stay upright, I lay back on the bed. "I guess that was too much."

"Aye, son," said my father. "A wee tad too much."

Then I think I slept some more.

When I awoke again, it was morning. Real morning this time, with the sunlight pouring through my window. I swung my feet slowly out of bed and cautiously stood up. The floor behaved itself and didn't sway and buckle like the last time I tried standing. But my legs were weak and my knees felt as if they were made of rubber. I sat back down on the bed, took a deep breath, and tried again.

This time I made it to the bedroom door and, taking another deep breath, ventured into the hallway. A few more faltering steps got me as far as the kitchen, where my mother saw me and came to take my arm.

"Ted! You should have called for me to come and help you."

"I don't need help, Ma," I said, but let her hold my arm and guide me to a chair anyway. "But I *am* hungry."

"A good sign," she said. She put a full glass of milk on the table in front of me. "Here, start with this and I'll fetch the rest of your breakfast. Doctor Wilkinson said you would be your-self by this morning, and he was right. You are much better."

"Yes, Ma. I'm sorry I caused you concern and made the doctor come to the house. He was here, wasn't he? I seem to remember that he and Pa made me walk and walk and walk."

Ma laughed. "They did indeed, son. And you grumbled and complained the whole time until Doctor Wilkinson declared you far too irritable to be in any further danger. So we put you back to bed to sleep to your heart's content."

"Sorry," I said again. I didn't remember complaining. Actually, I didn't remember much about yesterday at all.

I ate. When I next stood up my legs were steady and held me upright without difficulty. Ma brought hot water to my room, and I washed and dressed and then went back to the kitchen.

"Doctor Wilkinson will have to give me another bottle of laudanum," I said. "I won't take the whole of it tonight, just the dosage the doctor says. I'll have him write it down so there will be no misunderstanding. It served its purpose well, Ma. I did not have nightmares."

My mother shook her head. "I know that you did not dream while you slept, even though you were asleep for the better part of yesterday. But Doctor Wilkinson assured me that he will not, under any circumstances, ever prescribe laudanum for you again."

"Why not?"

"Ted, you did not see yourself yesterday. You were covered with a rash, all over your face and hands and chest, as if you had scarlet fever. We could not wake you, no matter how hard we tried."

"That's because I took too much of the medicine, Ma."

"It was not merely that, Ted. The doctor says that some people have a sensitivity to laudanum and it was that sensitivity, not just the fact that you took too much, which caused you to sleep so long and so deeply. Doctor Wilkinson believes that if you use it again your condition would worsen."

"I wasn't sick, just tired and I slept, *without* nightmares."

"I know that, son. But the price you paid for that dreamless sleep was far too high ... for all of us. We must find another method of dealing with your dreams, a method that does not involve medication."

There was a loud knock on the kitchen door. Ma opened it and J.B. came in. He grinned, clapping his hands enthusiastically when he saw me at the table. "Ah, you are awake enough to eat. Good. Has the floor stopped behaving as if it

41

were a boat in high seas?"

"Yes," I said. "I'm sorry I didn't pay closer attention to your instructions."

"No harm done, now that you are recovered, Ted. But has your mother told you that you must be extremely careful in the future to avoid any medication similar to laudanum? That is, anything which contains opium, its main ingredient."

"She told me," I said. "But I don't agree. It worked, J.B. I didn't dream about ... about *him* for the first time in months."

Ma had set a cup of coffee on the table, and the doctor sat down and pulled it towards him. "I can not prescribe another medication for you, Ted. I fear that something else might have an even worse effect. Drugs are not the answer."

He must have seen how disappointed I looked, for he laughed. Leaning back in his chair and tucking his thumbs under his suspenders he said, "Courage, Ted, courage. There are other ways of dealing with distressing dreams."

"What other ways?"

"You give up sleeping. There, the problem is solved."

"But, Doctor ..." said my mother.

"That's not ..." I began. Then I saw his grin. "You jest," I said.

"I do," he admitted. "It would be a good answer if it were possible, but since it is not, I have another suggestion."

"I am relieved to hear that," said my mother crossly. "This is no joking matter, Doctor Wilkinson. And please do not lean back in that manner; it will weaken the chair."

"I apologize sincerely, Mrs. MacIntosh," he said, straightening up and looking serious. "Please forgive me if I spoke inappropriately. Unfortunately I tend to do that far too often for my own good."

"What do you suggest, then?" I asked.

"I have a theory, Ted, that when the mind is kept busy during the day, it has no strength to formulate dreams at night. So I propose that for the next few months we keep your mind—and your body as well, for unfortunately science has not yet discovered a way to separate the two—occupied from sun-up to sun-down."

"But Theodore *is* busy all day, Doctor. He has his chores, he works with his father in the carpentry shop, he practises his violin and ..."

"Yes," agreed the doctor. "His hands are busy. But his mind is free to wander and wonder and worry. He needs work which involves his mind, allowing it no time to dwell on fears or fancies or fate. Or on Mr. James Barry."

"I can continue Ted's schooling," said Ma, and her eyes began to gleam. "Just last year the library was moved to Barkerville from Camerontown. It is much more convenient, and Mr. John Bowron, who serves as the librarian, reports that he now has over five hundred books in the collection. There is still much for Ted to learn."

"But, Ma," I said. "I know how to read and write *and* do sums. I do not need any more schooling."

"When you began to work with your father, I agreed to discontinue your instruction, Ted. But if you will not be learning carpentry, then I see no reason why we should not return to your lessons. Your knowledge of geography is far from adequate, and we have yet to study Mr. Tennyson's poetry."

"But, Ma ..."

"I will hear no arguments about it, Theodore. We shall begin work tomorrow morning." She tossed her head as she spoke, and her lips settled into a determined line.

I sighed. I knew that look well. In spite of my wishes, I suspected I would soon resume my studies. Some of the books Ma made me read were interesting, ones like *The Swiss Family Robinson*. But poetry? I didn't want to have to study poetry.

"J.B.," I pleaded. "That's not what you meant, was it? You didn't mean that I was to go back to lessons, did you?"

The doctor was quiet for a moment before he answered. "Mr. Tennyson, yes, I know his work; very good poetry but very *long* poetry. And Geography, of course. How about Mathematics? Is Ted's arithmetic schooling complete, Mrs. MacIntosh?"

"J.B.," I said again. "Please."

He laughed, and I realized that once again he was teasing. Ma realized it, too, and she spoke curtly.

"Well, if not with more lessons, Doctor, then how do you propose to keep Theodore's mind occupied so that he will not dream at night?"

"By having him by my side for most of the day and for some nights as well. It is common for doctors to take an apprentice, a young man who works with them and learns what he can about the profession before he undertakes the rigorous course of studies which will qualify him to be a doctor. I would like Ted to be my unofficial apprentice."

"Oh, my!" said my mother. She looked at Doctor Wilkinson, then at me, then back at the doctor again. "Oh, my!" she said again. "My son. A doctor."

"No, not a doctor, Mrs. MacIntosh, but rather a student, a helper, an assistant. I can not possibly teach Ted everything he needs to know, nor would it be legal. Why, just last year an ordinance was passed in New Westminster for all practitioners of medicine. A doctor must have at least three years of study at a college and be officially registered or he may not practise his profession in the Colony of British Columbia. Ted will learn some things from me, but much more study is needed before he can become a physician."

"It would be an honour if you would select Theodore as your assistant," my mother said. "I have always wished that there were a man of medicine in the family. Now, perhaps, that wish will come true. If ..." The smile left her face and she stared hard at the doctor.

"If what, Mrs. MacIntosh?" he asked, his own face as serious as hers. "If you consider me an appropriate mentor?"

"Well, yes. You must admit, Doctor Wilkinson, that you have had your troubles. A few years ago you were in considerable ... distress, were you not?"

"I was. At that time no mother would allow her son to work with me. Nor would I have considered taking on an apprentice. My heart was not in my work and I was, as you so considerately called it, in much distress."

"And now, Doctor?"

He pushed himself up from the chair, and went to my mother. Gently he put one hand on her arm, and looked her steadily in the eyes.

"Mrs. MacIntosh, my troubles are behind me and I promise that they shall not recur, not ever. I give you my word."

Ma put her hand over his. "It was a terrible time, both for you and for poor Mr. Cameron."

What was Ma talking about? I knew Mr. Cameron, 'Cariboo' Cameron people called him. But what had J.B. to do with him? And what was the 'trouble' Ma kept talking about? I had my mouth open, a question ready, but one look at my mother's face and I realized that this was not the best time to ask anything.

Ma disentangled her arm from J.B.'s grip. She held out her hand. J.B. took it and they shook hands solemnly. "I will hold you to your word, Doctor," she said.

"I will keep it. Then may I take Ted as my unofficial apprentice?"

"With my blessing, Doctor."

"Thank you. Then it is settled. I spoke to Mr. MacIntosh this morning, and he also has agreed. So, now that I have your approval, Mrs. MacIntosh, the deal is debated, decided and done. Ted, put on your boots and jacket and come with me. We'll start immediately."

"Excuse me," I said. "I don't recall expressing any desire to become a doctor or even a doctor's assistant."

"Nonsense, Theodore," said my mother in that tone of voice which meant that she had already made my decision for me. "It will be good for you to learn skills other than those your father can teach you. You do need something to occupy your mind."

"My mind is well occupied right now," I said. "I don't wish to work with J.B."

"But why not, Ted?" asked the doctor, looking both surprised and hurt at once. "I would enjoy spending more time in your company, and I had assumed the feeling was mutual."

I thought quickly. "It is just that I don't know what my duties would be," I said. "I can not help you with patients. What else is there to do?"

"You will keep the surgery and my instruments clean,"

said the doctor, "and help me keep written records of the diagnosis and treatment of each patient as well as their symptoms. You'll mix the powders and tinctures I prescribe—once you've learned the difference between a teaspoon and a tablespoon, that is. You will come with me on house calls when I need someone to handle the horse and buggy and ... Oh, there are many things for you to do."

"But I don't ..." I began, but no one was listening.

"Come along, Ted," said J.B. as he bid my mother good morning and started out the door.

There didn't seem to be anything else to do. I pulled on my boots, picked up my jacket, and nervously followed him.

Nervously, because I had a problem. J.B. didn't know about it yet, although he would find out soon enough. Ma believed I had outgrown it, but I hadn't. It was something which I was sure was not one of the qualifications which would make me a successful doctor's apprentice.

I faint at the sight of blood.

Four

"Welcome to my surgery," said J.B. He unlocked the door of a building between two stores on Barkerville's main street. "Come in, come in."

I hung up my jacket and pulled off my boots while the doctor stoked the fire in the wood stove. Although I had been tended to by doctors at home a time or two in the past, I had only once been inside a doctor's surgery, the time J.B. gave me the laudanum. I hadn't paid too much attention then, but now I looked around me with more curiosity. At first glance it seemed not unlike any other office, only J.B.'s black leather travelling bag indicated that this was where a doctor worked.

A roll top desk, open to show a dozen pigeonholes crammed with papers, was pushed up against one wall and two chairs were beside the desk. Both the desk and the chairs were covered with books—thin books, thick books, books with tattered covers, leather-bound books. There were piles of books everywhere, even stacked in a corner on the floor.

Close to the stove, beside a small table with a reading lamp, was a cushioned easy-chair with one broken leg. That chair, too, was piled with books; they overflowed onto the table, threatening to nudge the lamp over the edge. Where did J.B. expect his patients to sit, I wondered?

I picked up one of the books, a heavy one. *Anatomy of the Human Body* it said on the cover. "What is 'anatomy,' J.B.?"

"I don't think anatomy is the best subject to begin with," he said. "Perhaps we will start with something more suitable to your age. And more, I am certain, to your mother's liking." He took the book from my hand and tossed it back onto the chair. A cloud of dust puffed up around my face, and I sneezed.

J.B. looked around him as if he were seeing, for the first time, the books that filled the room. "I think that one of your duties will be to use your carpentry skills and build a bookshelf," he said. "I suspect that my patients sometimes find it disconcerting to perch on a pile of books—to perch, perhaps painfully, on plentiful piles ... Well, enough of that. To work, Ted."

I looked around me. "But what shall I do?" I asked, sneezing again. "Do you want me to start building the bookshelf now?"

"Certainly not. My consultation hours begin shortly and patients will not want to relate their symptoms against the noise of hammer blows. Or sneezes."

I sneezed once more. "Most odd," said J.B. "However, let us forget your sneezes for I have a suggestion as to how you can occupy your time. Come with me."

We went into a second room, smaller than the first one and even thicker in dust.

"Welcome to my dispensary," he said. "From this palatial room I dispense dosages for my patients, dreams for myself—

for, as you can see, this room is where I sleep—and dinner. Rarely dinner, for I am not a skilled cook."

Again I looked around me. Crammed into the room were a cook stove, a table covered with an assortment of pots, dishes and empty medicine bottles, and two wooden chests, the largest of them with drawers and a sturdy padlock.

There was also an unmade bed, the blankets bunched up at its foot, and one whole wall of hooks dangling layers of clothing. Two pairs of boots were lined up beneath the clothes, and suspenders and belts were draped over everything, forming a sort of net which, I hoped, served to hold all of the clothes securely and prevent them from tumbling to the ground.

"Perhaps I should also build you a wardrobe," I said and as I spoke a jacket slipped off the hook on which it was hung and fell to the ground. I tried to hang it back up, but only succeeded in dislodging a shirt and some long underwear.

J.B. took the clothing from my hands and replaced it carefully. "I maintain that wardrobes hinder your ability to find clothes," he said. "Rather than rummaging rigorously and randomly in a dark cupboard, I hang my clothes where I can see everything at a glance. Besides, although I agree that I am in need of the services of a carpenter, I thought that you were to be my medical helper."

"I don't mind building things for you," I said quickly. "I know more of carpentry than I do of medicine." I would avoid the blood if I could spend my apprenticeship hammering rather than bandaging, I thought hopefully.

J.B. grinned at me. "Perhaps you will do both. Remember, my intention is to fill you so full of new knowledge and skills that your fears will be pushed out of your busy mind, and your nightmares will end. That was our plan, was it not?"

"Yes," I admitted reluctantly and sneezed again, loudly.

"I suspect that a good sweeping and dusting will both cure your sneezes and immensely improve the condition of this room. When you have completed those tasks ..."

I interrupted before he could finish. *"Dusting?"* I asked, horrified. *"Sweeping?"*

"Yes," he said cheerfully. "First you sweep and then you dust and then ..." He pulled the smallest wooden chest to the centre of the room and flung open the lid. Inside were empty bottles and jars, dozens of them in all sizes, shapes and colours, heaped together so they filled the chest almost to the brim.

"I store these here for future use," he said. "When I prescribe a medication, I mix it from the ingredients I keep safely locked up in this other chest, then I scrounge for both a bottle and a stopper which fits it. That can be a lengthy process since the correct stopper always seems to be beneath everything else. Sometimes, by the time I have found the containers for the medicine, the patient's illness has worsened or, worse yet, he has grown impatient and left without his medication and without paying my fee."

I picked up a green bottle, much like the one J.B. had filled with my laudanum. It was dusty, and there was something dark nestled inside it. I turned the bottle upside down and jumped as a large spider fell out.

"Tincture of spider, essence of dust and, perhaps, infusion of mouse droppings," said the doctor, watching the spider scuttle across the floor. "Although I blow into the bottles before I fill them, to dislodge the dust and any large items which do not belong in my prescription, I am sure that more than one patient has swallowed fly wings along with their sulphur and molasses tonic."

"Or spider legs," I said, wondering if I had received a dose of insect limbs with my laudanum.

"You know, Ted, it occurs to me that *all* of my patients would benefit if you were to spend some time washing *all* of these containers."

"Washing?"

"Indeed. You are familiar with the term? Here." He handed me a bucket and placed a pot on the stove. "While I tend to patients, busy yourself by boiling water and thoroughly cleaning the contents of this treasure chest of mine. After you have swept and dusted, that is. This is a small room, the cleaning will not take long. Later, perhaps, you can install shelves so that my things can be stored more conveniently, but for now, Ted, set a fire, seize the broom and search diligently for cobwebs. But first you must fetch water from outside."

He grinned at me again and left the room. I picked up another bottle from the jumble in the chest and carefully turned it upside down. No more spiders emerged, but I was sure that I had not seen the last of them.

In the other room I heard the doctor greeting a patient, and then the thud of books hitting the floor as J.B. cleared a chair and offered it to the visitor. Their voices were low and, through the closed door, I could hear only faint mutterings. I sighed and, picking up the bucket, headed outside to the pump.

This was not the work I had expected a doctor's apprentice to do. This was *woman's* work.

The Doctor's Apprentice

My first few days as Doctor Wilkinson's apprentice were spent doing cleaning and more cleaning, much more than was to my liking. My mother laughed when I told her of my duties and scolded me for complaining.

"A man's work, a woman's work, it makes no difference, Ted. If there is a job to be done, then someone has to do it. Perhaps, if you need to practise your new skills, you could spend a few hours helping me with *my* spring cleaning."

J.B. didn't need spring cleaning. He needed it for fall, winter, and summer as well to make up for the years he had neglected to clean anything.

I washed every bottle and jar in his dispensary as well as the dishes, some of which looked as if they hadn't been near water since they were bought. For more than a week I swept, scrubbed, polished—and sneezed. I moved piles of books and dusted them and became more intimately acquainted with dirt, cobwebs, and even the occasional dead mouse than I had any wish to be.

With my father's help I built shallow shelves to store J.B.'s bottles and jars and an enormous bookshelf to keep his books off the floor and the furniture. I also put up more hooks for his clothing and moved the bed and the two trunks out of the way so I could scrub the floor with a strong solution of coal-tar soap and hot water. The dispensary and surgery gleamed. J.B. had even been persuaded to commission my father to build him a wardrobe and to repair the broken leg on his favourite chair.

My mother came to town and carried away all of the doctor's curtains to launder. She took a good look around her and announced that she had assumed that a medical man would

53

be cleaner and better organized, and she hoped that I, when I became a doctor, would have more sense than to let my lodgings fall into such disrepair.

J.B. thanked her for her help. "But you know, Mrs. MacIntosh, all medical students must pass an exam in disorderliness in order to qualify as doctors. We were severely penalized if our quarters were inspected and found to be clean and neat. I found it difficult, but I managed to avoid demerits for tidiness."

"A great personal sacrifice, I am sure, Doctor," said my mother, smiling at him. She had come to recognize his tone of voice when he was joking, and was no longer taken in by his teasing.

With J.B.'s surgery and living quarters clean and organized, I spent the next week of my apprenticeship with my nose buried in books. Not the one about anatomy (J.B. had told me to leave that subject alone for now), but books about medicines, herbs, concoctions, and chemicals and their use in the treatment of illnesses.

I *did* learn the difference between a teaspoon and a tablespoon, also between a pint and a quart, and an ounce and a dram. I learned that when you added a minim of something to a mixture, you added barely a drop and that when an ingredient was to be finely ground the mortar and pestle would reduce it to a powder with only a little effort. By the end of my second week, I was allowed to mix some of the prescriptions myself, at first nervously supervised by J.B., then entirely on my own.

I was also given the job of writing out all of J.B.'s instructions, detailing how the medicines he dispensed should be

taken, and soon memorized the spelling of such words as laudanum, bicarbonate, quinine, and camphor. I learned how
each was used to ease pain, relieve gas, bring down a high
fever, or take away the itch of insect bites.

In my measuring and mixing, my hands became stained
yellow from the fine powder called 'flowers of sulphur,' pur-
ple from solutions of potassium permanganate and blotched
white from splashes of carbolic acid. The carbolic acid was
mixed with water into a solution which J.B. had recently
begun using to clean both his hands and a patient's wounds
after reading a newly published paper by Doctor Lister which
recommended it. My mother sighed when she saw my hands,
and insisted on vigorous washing before she would let me sit
at the table to eat, even though I assured her that those were
stains, not dirt, and scrubbing would not help.

I learned so much and worked so hard that when I crawled
into my bed at night my head was crammed with words:
names and terms and measurements. I would dream of how
to mix sulphur and molasses for a tonic, of how much peppermint essence to put into a baby's colic medicine, of how to
count the drops of opium when making a tincture of laudanum.

I read. I memorized. I wrote dosage instructions, mixed
medications, and kept both the surgery and the dispensary
clean. Doctor Wilkinson had been right. I had no room in
my head for nightmares. I did not dream of James Barry, in
fact I seldom even thought of him.

Five

I had been J.B.'s assistant for almost a month when, shortly before my fourteenth birthday, I went with him to visit a patient.

The call for the doctor came one day near the end of May as J.B. and I were eating our noon meal in Wake up Jake's. Although I received no pay for my duties as his helper, J.B. made sure that my stomach was well filled.

A young woman approached our table. "Doctor," she said, "will you come with me, please?" I recognized her, although I didn't remember her name. She was a chambermaid at The Hotel de France, and I had seen her when she had come to Pa's shop to fetch him. Pa often went to the hotels to do small repairs to furniture, rather than having the damaged piece brought to his shop.

"Ah, Bridget," said J.B. He seemed to know everyone's name. "Sit down. Join Ted and me for some victuals."

"No, thank you kindly, Doctor. It's about Mrs. Fraser. She's ... it's her time and it's her first." Bridget blushed and looked down at her feet, avoiding my eyes. "The foolish woman has locked the door to her room, Doctor, and will let no one near her. She only weeps and calls for her husband."

"He won't be much help to her now," said J.B.

Bridget blushed again. "The Frasers are new to town; they arrived by stagecoach two weeks ago. Her husband has gone to Wingdam where he hopes to buy a claim, and she has been alone all week. She keeps to herself; she's no older than I am, yet she puts on airs as if she were a fine lady and could not possibly associate with the likes of me."

"That will be her great loss, my dear," said J.B., smiling at her. "Perhaps, however, she is merely shy."

She smiled back at him. "That is possible. But wouldn't you think that any woman great with child would welcome friendship, no matter how shy she might be?"

"With child?" I asked. "You mean she's ..."

Bridget blushed again and looked down at the floor, but J.B. answered me. "Yes, Ted. I believe that Barkerville will have a new inhabitant before the day is out."

"Will you come, Doctor?" asked Bridget again. "Perhaps you can persuade her to unlock the door. I have helped with all three of my sister's children. I know what to do if she will let me."

"Certainly, Bridget. We'll come with you."

"We?" I asked.

"Yes, Ted. You are young and personable. If I can not persuade Mrs. Fraser to unlock the door and allow me to help with the delivery, you will have to try. We can not leave the poor woman all alone to give birth to her first child, can we?"

"Me? You mean you want me to—"

"Come along, Ted. Don't dawdle. Put aside your food, you can eat later. The baby will not wait until your stomach

57

is satisfied, whereas your daily bread—or beans, bacon and bannock," he added, after a look at my meal, "will keep safely until we are finished."

"Baby? But I know nothing of—"

"Stop procrastinating. There will be much for you to do, especially since you have become so skilled at boiling water. Bridget and I can use the help of an extra pair of hands, isn't that so, Bridget?"

She giggled. "Him? Young Ted? Oh, he will be of much help, I am sure! He is but a child himself."

I stood up. "I am not a child," I announced. "I am Doctor Wilkinson's apprentice, and soon to be a medical man myself. And I am nearly fourteen."

"Quite old enough to help deliver a baby," said J.B. "Definitely quite old enough." He pushed his plate away from him. "Lead on, fair Bridget."

Looking back regretfully at my unfinished meal, I followed them. I *was* hungry, but I was also worried, not only about my role in the delivery of Mrs. Fraser's baby, but about J.B. as well. I wondered if he was ill—he seemed to be trying to hold back a violent attack of coughing and something was wrong with his left eye. It twitched violently whenever he looked at Bridget.

I had seen many of J.B.'s patients at his surgery, had even helped him when he needed an extra pair of hands to hold an inebriated miner while a broken bone was being set and again when he sewed up a knife wound. I no longer fainted at the sight of blood and considered myself an accomplished assistant, but I had never accompanied the doctor on any of his visits to patients' homes. This was my first "house call."

"This way, Doctor. It's the front room on the second floor. Hurry." J.B. and I followed Bridget up a narrow flight of stairs and down the hotel's long hallway. It was quiet in the building and dark in the windowless corridor. I waited nervously while Bridget knocked and called, "Mrs. Fraser? I've brought the doctor for you, ma'am."

There was no answer but something heavy thudded against the closed door, causing me to jump back.

"Now, Mrs. Fraser," said Bridget. "It will do you no good to throw things. The doctor is here. Open the door."

"Go away," said a small voice from the room. "Leave me alone. I don't want anyone with me. Go away."

Bridget shrugged her shoulders and turned to J.B. "That one has a temper, she does!"

"Let me try," said J.B. and he knocked on the door himself. "Mrs. Fraser? Please open the door. I am Doctor Wilkinson and I can assure you that I have delivered many babies. I will be able to help you if you will open the door and allow me to enter the room."

There was another thud against the door and the sound of glass shattering. Then silence.

"See what I mean, Doctor?" said Bridget. "She is no longer calling for her husband, but I suspect that was a lamp which she just threw at us."

"Luckily, the lamp appears not to have been lit," said J.B., sniffing the air. "I do not smell burning, do you? However, I agree that Mrs. Fraser seems most reluctant to accept help."

"Then perhaps we can go and finish our meal?" I said, hopefully. "If she won't open the door, then we're of no use here."

J.B. looked at me and smiled. "Childbirth can be an unsettling experience for many women," he said. "We can not leave her alone in this state."

"But if she won't allow us to enter the room ..." I began, then from behind the closed door there suddenly came the sound of someone panting, their breath coming in fast, shallow gasps as if they had just run a long and tiring race.

J.B. listened for a moment, then turned to Bridget. "Unlock the door," he said. "You do have a master key, don't you? Use it, quickly. I suspect Mrs. Fraser is too busy right now to care if we enter her chamber without her permission. Hurry, lass. We are needed in there."

Bridget took a large key ring from her pocket, selected a key and unlocked the door. The doctor disappeared inside the room, and Bridget followed. I stood in the doorway wondering if Mrs. Fraser were still intent on throwing things in this direction.

"J.B. What shall I do now?"

"We've no time for you, Ted," said Bridget. "Go away."

The window curtains were drawn, and it was dark in the room. I could barely see J.B. standing beside the bed. He looked up at me, and I think he smiled.

"It's all right, Ted," he said. "I was only joking when I said that your help would be needed to deliver the baby. Bridget and I—and Mrs. Fraser—can handle the situation. But if you wish to be of assistance, you could find the kitchen and fetch us hot water. Also clean rags, towels, sheets, anything they'll let you have. Bring them back here, and then stay out of the way."

I could hear Bridget's voice, soft and gentle, and the doctor's reassuring words. Over both of their voices rose the sound of panting, louder now, louder and faster, and once in a while I thought I heard a cuss word shouted in a woman's voice. I shut the door and went in search of hot water, unsure whether I felt anger or relief.

I was relieved, I finally decided. Definitely relieved.

When I found the hotel's kitchen, the cook already had a large kettle of water nearing the boil. "Ah," she said when she saw me. "So the doctor has come at last. About time, if you ask me."

"I need—" I started to say, but she didn't let me finish.

"Sit down," she said. "There's a pot of tea on the stove. I'll pour you a cup—you look as if you could do with something warm in your stomach. You're looking peaked, Master Ted, if I do say so."

"But I have to take the hot water—"

"In a while, but not yet. You've time for a cup of tea and a slice of bread and preserves before you'll be needed up there. Babies take their time coming, especially the first ones. You'll just be in the way, like as not. Sit down, sit down."

I sat down and guiltily drank tea, ate two slices of bread, then the cook let me go. She handed me the kettle of hot water, tucked a bundle of clean rags under my arm, grinned and sent me away.

"Don't worry," she said. "The first one is always the hardest. Soon you'll be doing the doctor's work and he'll be down here with me, sipping tea."

Bridget came into the hall shortly after I arrived back upstairs. "It's a boy," she said. "Have you brought something to wash the wee thing with?"

I handed her the rags and the water. "A baby?" I said. "A baby boy?"

"And what did you think it would be," said Bridget as she disappeared back into the room. "A baby moose?"

I hear J.B. laugh, and then a thin, small sound, rather like a cat mewling for a dish of cream. For a while the room was silent except for the low voices of J.B. and Bridget.

Then all at once Mrs. Fraser's ragged breathing began again, growing louder and faster. J.B. shouted at Bridget, Bridget yelled back at him, and the bedroom door swung open.

"Lord help us, there's another one coming," Bridget gasped, rushing towards me. "Here, take this." She thrust the bundle of rags at me and dashed back into the room. The bundle squirmed in my hands and made a small, cat-like noise. I was holding a baby.

I held it out in front of me, rather as if I were carrying a tray, and stared at it. The baby opened its eyes and stared back. It didn't look much like any small child I had ever seen before. Although it had the right number of eyes and ears, it had no hair at all and its skin was red and wrinkled-looking. It moved again, and I held it tightly, afraid it would squirm right out of my grasp. I must have gripped it too hard, because its face twisted into a strange grimace, its eyes shut tightly, its mouth opened, and it began to cry.

"Hush," I said, bouncing it up and down in my arms. "Please, hush."

It did no good. The infant squealed louder. How could I

ever have thought that the noises coming out of that toothless mouth sounded like a kitten—the cries were much louder than any cat that I had ever heard.

"Quiet," I said. "Please, don't cry." I looked at it balanced on my hands, and suddenly a tiny hand found its way free of the covers. It was so small, so very small. The largest fingernail on that hand seemed hardly larger that a grain of rice.

"Poor thing," I thought, and I pulled it to me and held it against my chest, cradling it the way I had seen women hold their babies. The crying stopped, and for what seemed like a long time I rocked the child and watched it sleep peacefully in my arms.

"Now who taught you how to tend to wee ones, Ted? You've a gentle touch—look, the babe is sleeping."

I looked up. "He's so small, J.B. I didn't know babies were this tiny. He hardly weighs anything."

"To his mother's great relief," he answered. "She would have found it far more difficult to carry two large babies than two tiny ones. But let me take him. He needs to go and meet his brother, and his mother is anxious to see him. She didn't have much of a chance to get formally acquainted."

Almost reluctantly I handed the baby over to him. "Come with me," he said. "Mrs. Fraser wants to meet you, too."

"Me? Why?"

"Ask her yourself."

I followed J.B. into the room, nervously keeping an eye open for flying objects. But although my boots crunched on shards of glass from the broken chimney of an oil lamp, Mrs. Fraser no longer seemed inclined to hurl objects in my direction.

"Go ahead," said J.B., motioning me towards the bed. I moved slowly forward.

Mrs. Fraser was a young woman, much younger than I had imagined. I'd always thought of mothers as being, well, older. Like Ma. But Mrs. Fraser looked not much more than my age. She lay back against the bed pillows, one child beside her. J.B. handed her the baby I had held and she kissed it, then tucked it into the curve of her other arm and smiled.

"They're beautiful," she said.

"Indeed, they are certainly a couple of comely children, Mrs. Fraser. Your husband will be proud."

"When he overcomes his surprise at seeing *two* he will be," said Mrs. Fraser. She had red hair, curly and tangled, and it lay on the pillow around her face. Her skin was very pale, and she had many freckles, a great many. She smiled at me.

"This is Ted MacIntosh," said J.B. "He is my assistant."

"Thank you for your help, Ted," she said. "Doctor Wilkinson assured me that his assistant was caring for my firstborn. I did not know that you were either so young or so red-headed."

"Now that you mention it," said J.B., studying me, "Ted looks enough like you to be your brother, Mrs. Fraser."

"He does at that!" said Bridget. "Red hair and freckles, and even their eyes are the same."

"I wish you were my brother," said Mrs. Fraser. "My husband and I have no kin in this country, and I miss my family. Perhaps we are related, Ted. There have been MacIntoshes in my family, although several generations ago."

"My parents are from Inverness," I said.

"Mine too," she said and smiled. She looked tired and pale, but when she smiled her face seemed to glow.

"You must meet Ted's parents," said J.B. "Once you are up and about I shall introduce you and your husband to them. Perhaps you have found kinfolk in the goldfields after all."

"I hope so," she said. "I feel less lonely already."

"You will scarcely have time to be lonely now," said Bridget. "Not with those two to care for. What will you call them?"

"I think I will name them after their godfathers," said Mrs. Fraser, smiling. "That is, if Ted and Doctor Wilkinson will accept the positions."

"Godfather? Me?"

"I think Ted means that he would be honoured, Mrs. Fraser. As would I, of course."

"Then they shall carry your names," she said. "Doctor, I know your first name is 'John' but I am not fond of that name. Also, my husband has an uncle named 'Theodore'—that is what 'Ted' is short for, isn't it—who has the meanest temper of any man alive. I would not wish his name on a child of mine. But perhaps you both have second given names which will suit. Tell me, what are your middle names?"

"Our middle names?" said J.B.

"The middle ones?" I said.

"That is what she asked," said Bridget. "Your middle names. What is wrong with the two of you? Do you not understand?"

I didn't know what to say, but Bridget did. "I believe I have heard Ted referred to as Master Per ..." she began.

"Robert," I said, interrupting her. "Robert is a good name." Bridget looked surprised.

J.B. nodded. "Robert is a grand name," he said. "As for me, I have always liked 'Andrew.' I would be content if one child were to be called Andrew."

"Both are good Scottish names," said Mrs. Fraser. "It is settled, then. Robert and Andrew their names shall be."

"Very distinguished names they are, too," said J.B. "An
excellent choice, Mrs. Fraser, if I do say so myself. Don't you
agree, Ted?"

"Uh ... yes."

They were fine names, but they weren't ours.

Six

"*R*obert?" asked J.B. The doctor and I had returned to Wake Up Jake's where we ordered another meal. I saw no reason to tell J.B. that I had been fed in the Hotel de France's kitchen, because I was hungry enough to eat again. "Robert?" he repeated.

"*Andrew?*" I asked him in return. "Your middle name begins with the letter 'B' and 'Andrew' definitely does not."

"Nor is 'Robert' the accepted short form of Per ... your middle moniker."

"I never claimed that Robert was my name, only that I thought it a good name. I did not lie."

"Nor did I," said J.B. "Although I confess that I found it a difficult situation. I, too, perched on the precipice of prevarication."

"*Why* must you do that?"

"Do what?"

"Speak that way."

"Ah, Ted, I am merely indulging a whim of mine. Besides, I hope that I am improving your vocabulary."

"My vocabulary does not need your help. I understand

many difficult words, but must you always use them when you talk? Such as 'perched on the precipice of pre ...' whatever that other word meant."

"Prevarication means lying."

"I don't care! I wish you would just speak the way a normal person does."

"I am sorry if it offends you," said J.B. He looked surprised. "I had no idea that you found my speech patterns such an aimless and annoying attribute."

I glared at him. "You're doing it again."

"So I am. I apologize. I do not mean to cause you distress."

"It doesn't distress me," I said, reluctantly. "At least it doesn't most of the time. But just now it seemed ... I don't know why it made me angry. I'm sorry I spoke harshly."

He smiled at me. "The birth of a child is an emotional time, both for the parents and for those who are present. I always find it ..."

His voice trailed off. Our food came and I ate heartily, making up for the meal I had left on the table when we rushed off. I was too busy eating to talk much, but when I had finished I realized that J.B. was unusually quiet. He had only picked at his food, and much of it was untouched.

"J.B.? You have not spoken a word for the whole meal. Are you angry at me?"

"What? No, Ted, I am not angry."

"Then what is wrong? Do you feel sick?"

"No, my body is perfectly healthy." He sighed, then pushed away his plate. "It is my thoughts and memories which distress me. I fear that tonight I shall dream."

"Dream of what?" I asked. "Surely you do not suffer from

nightmares. You are a doctor; you know best how to cure yourself of upsetting dreams. Besides, you are a grown man and night terrors are things only children suffer."

"Ah, you are wrong on both counts. It is a rare physician who can heal himself, and the world of nightmares belongs as much to adults as to those much younger." He sighed again. "The birth of the twins, an event which sharpened your tongue, will prompt my dreams. I know that an uneasy sleep awaits me tonight."

I looked at him, astonished. "You *do* have nightmares? As I do, or as I used to? But I dreamed of a murderer and a hanging; how can those tiny babies cause nightmares?"

The doctor stared at the table for a long time, not answering. In the two months I had worked for him, I had never known him to be silent for so long. I was worried for him and, in spite of his reassurances, not at all sure that he wasn't angry at me.

He raised his head and I could see that there were lines on his face which had not been there earlier in the day. He seemed to have aged ten years. There were deep creases bracketing his mouth, dark circles under his eyes, and two furrows between his eyebrows. He did not look angry; he looked sick and old.

"J.B., you are not well. Come back to the surgery. You need rest and perhaps a tonic ..."

He tried to smile at me. "Doctor Ted. Only a few short weeks of apprenticeship, and already you prescribe treatment. However, in this case your advice is sound and I shall follow it. If I can prevail upon you to accompany me? I know it grows late and your mother will expect you home shortly, but I confess I feel a great need for the company of a friend."

At the surgery he sat down in the easy chair and I busied myself lighting a fire. "A cup of tea would do you good," I said. "Or shall I brew some coffee?"

J.B. shook his head, but did not answer. I lit the lamps, turning up the wicks to their brightest, then set a kettle of water on the stove anyway, in case he should change his mind and ask for a hot drink. Then I pulled up one of the other chairs and sat facing him.

Between us the stove cracked and hissed as some pitch burst into flame, and the kettle began to sing softly to itself as it neared the boil. J.B. sat with his head bowed, his tall body almost doubled over on itself, one hand held to his forehead so his eyes were shaded. Then, his voice muffled and so soft I had to strain to hear his words, he began to tell me his story.

"Sophia Cameron was her name," he said. "They called her husband 'Cariboo'. Cariboo Cameron."

"I know of him. Camerontown is named for him," I said, but J.B. seemed not to hear me.

"I was Mrs. Cameron's doctor," he said, "It was I who delivered her child, born here in the goldfields only months after she and her husband arrived. It was I who brought that child into the world, and it was I who stood by its grave after Cariboo and I buried it."

"The baby died?" I asked.

"It was the second child Sophia had lost," J.B. went on. "The first died on the long journey here, died before she ever set foot in Barkerville, a place she soon came to despise."

"She was young. Before her marriage she had lived a sheltered life with her family. Life in the goldfields was not sheltered, nor refined, and she hated living here. Cariboo had invested in a gold claim, but although he and his partners toiled for long hours, working themselves to the point of exhaustion, the claim produced barely enough to buy the food they needed.

"Sophia was lonely. She had no relatives here, and she was not used to the difficulties of life in the goldfields: the primitive cabin, the bitter cold of winter, the lack of other women of her class to befriend. She yearned desperately to go back to her home in Ontario. She often spoke of her life there, of the small farm her father owned, and of the brilliant colours of the trees in autumn.

"I was her doctor, and I became her friend. Her only friend. Yet after the child died, it seemed that Sophia no longer wanted my friendship. Perhaps she blamed me for the baby's death. Perhaps she mourned, both for it and for the one who died before, mourned so greatly that she had no space left in her heart for friends. As she turned from me, I, not realizing her despair, abandoned her. I did not realize how much she suffered. I thought only that I had displeased her.

"So I left her alone, refusing even to tend to her in my professional capacity. There were other doctors in the goldfields, I thought. Let one of them deal with Sophia's complaints and tears and unfriendly behaviour. I had had enough of her coldness.

"Cariboo Cameron sought me out, told me of his wife's pitiful condition and of her desperate yearning to return to the home of her youth. She would not see another physician, he said, although she grew more despondent every day. He urged me to come to her, but I refused, dismissing his concerns.

"I told him that a woman's moods were not like a man's. 'She mourns for her dead children,' I said. 'It is natural and it will pass. It is nothing.'

"I did, however, give Cariboo laudanum to help his wife sleep, and urged him to have her drink spruce tea, a remedy I learned about from the Shuswap people who live near Soda Creek. Spruce tea, they told me, will lift the spirits as well as improve health. Cariboo Cameron offered his wife laudanum and many pots of spruce tea, but Sophia would not take them. I sent her tonics; she refused those as well.

"Yet of all the medicines I prescribed for Sophia Cameron, I did not offer her the most potent medicine of all—friendship.

"On October 22, 1862, she died. It was thirty degrees below zero, too cold for October, too cold even for Barkerville where winter comes so early. The wind howled and the snow ran before it, forming into drifts which would not melt until May. It was a dreadful day to die.

"The ground was frozen too deeply for a grave to be dug, so once a coffin was ready, her husband laid her to rest under the floorboards of an abandoned miner's cabin.

"It was a small group who gathered to bid Sophia goodbye. Although thousands lived on Williams Creek in the summer, there were very few who stayed here through that harsh winter. Not even a hundred people came to pray for Sophia at her funeral."

The fire had burned down and needed replenishing, but I didn't feel as if I should move. J.B. sat motionless, his head bowed. My feet were cold, I should add more wood to the fire and trim the lamps, I thought. One of the wicks was smoking and the lamp's chimney was turning black.

I didn't move until J.B. did. Finally he raised his head and looked at me as if he were seeing me for the first time.

"Stoke the fire, Ted, and then go home. I have talked at you for too long; it is late. Your mother will be worried."

I threw more logs into the stove, tended to the lamps, then picked up my jacket. But before I left there was something I had to ask, something I needed to know.

"J.B.? What do you see in your dreams? What frightens you?"

"I frighten myself," he said. "For in my dreams I see Sophia, her dead baby in her arms, her other child grasping her skirt. She holds out a hand to me, pleading, asking for my help, for my friendship. Night after night I see her reaching for my hand, and night after night I turn my back on her.

"Sophia Cameron is not the spectre which haunts me, Ted. I am my own nightmare; I am my own terror. From that there is no escape."

Seven

There was no moon and it was full dark by the time I left the doctor. As I walked through the streets of Barkerville the lamps from within the houses cast enough light so that travel was easy, but by the time I reached the end of town and began to climb the long hill which led to Richfield and my home, there was not a glimmer of light anywhere. I think that it was only because I had made this trip so often, because I knew the way so well, that I did not stumble and fall or wander off the path and plunge down the steep banks of Williams Creek. I walked slowly, my feet cautious on the road, but I wished to run, to ignore the ruts and grooves under my feet which might trip me, and run as fast as I could until I reached home.

It was darker than I had ever known a night to be. Although I was a doctor's assistant, a godfather to a baby, and almost fourteen, I was frightened. Perhaps it was J.B.'s talk of death and coffins which had put the fear back into me, but I felt terror as I had only known it in my dreams, a fear which brings with it a pounding heart and a cold clammy sweat on the brow. Then, as I neared the spot where I had

74

first seen James Barry, I saw him again.

Not physically, not in the flesh, but in my mind. In the dark I felt James Barry's presence. I knew that when I walked in front of that tree, just ahead around the bend in the road, I would hear his laughter once more.

There was a noise, a rustle in the bushes, the sound of something moving on the edge of the trail. I stood still and listened, but I heard nothing more. I took a deep breath and shouted, "Be gone. Whoever ... I mean, whatever you are, leave me alone." Then someone spoke.

"Ted, is that you?"

I could not move. I could not breathe. My heart leapt in my chest as if it, too, wished to escape.

"Ted, if that is you, answer me. Here, I have a lantern, but it has gone out. I'll light it again."

There was the scratch of a match, then a flash of light which steadied into a soft glow. A man's figure moved slowly into view, the lamp casting enough light so I could recognize his face.

"Pa!"

"Is that you, Ted? Your mother was worried for you, so she sent me out to search."

I found that I could breathe once more, so filled my lungs with air and felt my heart begin to slow. I took a step towards my father, then another one, then almost ran until I stood beside him.

"You are very late, son. Were there problems? I understand that you went to attend Mrs. Fraser and her twins. But I left the carpentry shop early tonight, and heard no more of your doings."

"It was not Mrs. Fraser who delayed me tonight. J.B. asked me to stay with him. He felt a need to talk, to tell me of ..." I thought quickly. Perhaps I should not tell my father what J.B. had told me. "He needed to discuss some things with me," I finished.

"I hope the doctor's trouble is not back with him," said my father. "Did he speak to you of Mrs. Cameron?"

"Yes," I said, surprised. "I didn't know that you knew about her."

"Everyone knows the story, and Doctor Wilkinson's role in it," he said. "However, we never spoke of it in front of children, so you would not have heard the tale. But it is well known that the doctor grieved deeply when Mrs. Cameron died, that he blamed himself. I had hoped that he had recovered, that he was not ..." He stopped speaking, and we walked in silence for a while. Somewhere an owl called, a lonesome sound. I moved closer to my father's side.

"That he was not *what?*" I asked at last. "I don't understand, Pa. J.B. has nightmares, is that what you mean?"

"Aye, nightmares, that does not surprise me. But there is more, son. Doctor Wilkinson will tell you someday, I have no doubt."

Ahead of us a splash of light from the lamp my mother had placed in the front window spilled out across the road, a beacon in the dark welcoming me home. I wanted to run, to push open the door to my house and close it tightly behind me, leaving the darkness and the ghosts shut outside. I quickened my steps, hurrying, and realized that I was hungry. Perhaps Ma would have saved me some biscuits from dinner. Maybe there would be warm soup or even stew. I was hungry, but hungry as much for the warmth and safety of my own home as for food.

But just before I reached the front door, I stopped. Something Pa had said was disturbing me. Something about Doctor Wilkinson.

"Pa," I asked. "What is wrong with J.B.? What did you mean about his trouble starting again?"

My father sighed, and bent down to blow out the lantern he carried. "You will find out soon enough if his trouble returns. But let us all hope that it never will."

I slept late the next morning, but awoke feeling tired. I hadn't dreamed, at least not that I remembered, but my eyes were heavy and I found it difficult to get out of bed. J.B. had told me not to come to work. "I have kept you away from home for a long time tonight, listening to me talk," he said. "Stay home for a day. Help your ma. I will manage without your assistance."

"I shall welcome some leisure tomorrow," I said. "It is my birthday."

"Ah, is it? I hadn't realized that. Please accept my best wishes and enjoy yourself."

My parents had not been pleased last night when I told them of my plans.

"You should go to work anyway, Ted," said my father. "It may be that the doctor needs you."

"He said he would not. Besides, tomorrow is my birthday."

"I am well aware of that, and I wish you many happy returns, as does your mother. However, you should go to work."

I was disappointed. "But J.B. said—"

"Doctor Wilkinson says many foolish things, son. I'm sure he did not mean it. I know you will be needed."

"I agree," said my mother firmly.

Although I had slept several extra hours I was still tired this morning, and also disappointed. I didn't want to make the trip to town. It was my birthday; surely I deserved a holiday. I would stay home, no matter what my parents said. But when I went for my breakfast, Ma had other plans.

"I have supplies which need to be purchased," she said. "You can fetch them for me and, while you are in town, check with Doctor Wilkinson to see if he needs you."

"I don't wish to check with him," I said.

"Theodore ..." said Ma, her voice sharp.

"I will go, if you insist," I said. "However, I don't understand why you and Pa are so eager for me to return to work when J.B. has said that—"

"Regardless of what the doctor told you, it would be a courtesy, Theodore. Besides, I need you to fetch my supplies; sugar and flour, things which are too heavy for me to carry. I will hear no more about it. Spend the morning at home if you wish, however after your noon meal I want you to go. But please tell the doctor that I want you home early."

In the afternoon, I went to town. I knew that it was useless to argue with Ma when she had that look on her face. It would be less trouble just to do as she wished.

I took my time, making the journey last as long as possible. Only when I passed the spot on the road where my father had found me last night, and when I walked by the Peace House in the Chinese section of Barkerville, did I push myself to move quickly. It didn't seem fair. I had been given a day of freedom, and not only were my parents refusing to allow me to enjoy it, but they neglected to take any notice at all of my birthday.

I stopped by Moses's shop after I had done Ma's shopping. Since J.B. wasn't expecting me today, he would not notice if I were late arriving. I would visit with Moses and tell him that I was a godfather. Maybe Moses would know what a godfather was supposed to do. Did I need to give baby Robert a gift? Was I responsible for making sure that the child had sufficient clothing and food and toys?

I realized that I had not told my parents of my new status; Ma would know what a godparent's role was, but she had been in a peculiar mood this morning.

The barbershop was closed, the blinds drawn and a sign on the door said that Mr. W.D. Moses would not be available to customers for the rest of the day. It was only three o'clock. Why had Moses closed so early?

I knocked on the door and called for him, just in case he were in the back room. No one answered.

J.B.'s surgery was closed, too. His sign said, "Patients with persistent and pertinent problems please present yourselves at a later period." The notice which J.B. usually placed on his door when he was unavailable simply said "Returning as soon as possible." I had never seen this sign before.

I went to Pa's shop. It was locked, the door bolted and the shades securely drawn. On the door was tacked a sign which said, "Closed this afternoon."

But that couldn't be! I had seen Pa leave for work this morning, and his shop had been open just now when I passed it on my way to do Ma's shopping. What had happened?

Perhaps he was at the restaurant, I thought, and headed for Wake Up Jake's. J.B. wasn't there, nor was Moses or my father. I hadn't really expected to see Pa there. He always said that it was foolish to spend good money on a meal when he could bring his food with him from home. However, I had been positive I would find the doctor at his usual table. But when I inquired about J.B.'s whereabouts, the proprietor just smiled and said he had no idea, as he hadn't seen Doctor Wilkinson since noon.

"And Mr. Moses?" I asked. "Have you seen him today? He hasn't taken ill, has he?"

"Not at all, Master Ted. He had some engagement this afternoon, but he is in perfect health, I assure you."

I picked up Ma's parcels and went home. No one was obliged to keep me informed of their activities, but I felt neglected. Since they had all seemingly found better things to do than work this afternoon, I would go home. Alone.

The sacks of sugar and flour which Ma had insisted I purchase were heavy, and I made the trip back up the hill almost as slowly as I had travelled on my trip to town. My arms ached from carrying the parcels, my feet felt heavy and moved reluctantly. I walked up the short path to our front door feeling out of sorts and irritable and, I suppose, slightly sorry for myself. After all, it was my birthday, and no one seemed to care.

I had been away from home for several hours, yet I had accomplished nothing except Ma's shopping. A waste of time, I thought. I could have stayed home, enjoyed my day with nothing to do.

One of J.B.'s words popped into my mind. *Disgruntled*. That was exactly how I felt—in bad humour, irritable and discontent.

I was definitely disgruntled as I pushed open the front door and stepped inside. Ma did not come to greet me, but as I took off my boots I heard a fiddle being played, softly at first, then louder and louder. Who was playing? What was that tune?

Then voices joined with the violin notes. "For he's a jolly good fellow, for he's a jolly good fellow, for he's a jolly good fellow ... and so say all of us."

"Happy birthday, Theodore! Come into the parlour. There are some friends of yours here to help you celebrate." Ma had changed from her work clothes into a dress she only wears for special occasions, and she was not wearing her apron. She hugged me. "Come in, son, we're waiting for you. Did you suspect that everyone had forgotten your birthday?"

"Not everyone," said J.B. as I stepped into the parlour. "Just me. When I told Ted to stay home and rest today, I had forgotten that his mother was counting on him being at work so that she could finish preparations for this celebration. I fear she was somewhat annoyed with me." The doctor looked tired, but he smiled and spoke cheerfully. I hoped he had not had nightmares last night after all.

J.B. was sitting on the sofa, Moses beside him. Mr. Malanion stood behind them holding his violin and my father sat in the wing back chair, smiling.

"Aye," said Pa. "You were not in Jeannie's good graces this morning, Doctor, but we managed to get Theodore out of the way without your help. By the expression on his face, we have succeeded in surprising him."

"You have," I said. "I was looking for you, J.B., and for Moses and Pa. It is no wonder I could not find you. And Mr. Malanion, it is good to see you again. I have not had much time for music lessons lately."

"It was planned that you not find us," said Moses. "We gathered at your father's shop, and the moment you passed on your way into Barkerville, we set out. We have been waiting for you to return."

"Which you finally have so now we can eat!" said J.B.

"Your good mother insisted that we wait for you before she would serve the meal, so we have been anxiously, ardently, and avidly awaiting your arrival. Excuse me, Ted. I meant to say that I am very pleased to see you for I am excessively hungry."

The table had been laid with the lace tablecloth that had belonged to my grandmother, and Ma had set out the best dishes. "Take your places, gentlemen," she said. "I have everything ready, in spite of my son's presence all morning."

Pa had opened a bottle of the chokecherry cordial Ma makes each summer, and he poured a glass for everyone, even me. My mother brought the serving platters and put them on the table, then she also sat down.

"To Theodore," said Moses, raising his glass. "He was my friend when he was a child and remains a friend as he moves into adulthood. To Ted."

Everyone lifted their glasses and said, "Ted," except for Ma, whose voice quavered as she added, "Happy birthday, son. You have grown up so fast, so fast."

"Thank you," I said. I no longer felt the least bit disgruntled; I felt exactly the opposite. Gruntled? "Thank you, everyone. Ma, can we eat? I'm starving."

J.B. agreed with me, loudly, and soon Pa had carved the meat and passed the plates to Ma who filled them with roast potatoes and fresh greens. She had made gravy, too, and biscuits, and opened a jar of her special rhubarb, onion and raisin relish.

"To Ted," said Mr. Malanion, raising his glass to me again. My father noticed that it was empty, and uncorked another bottle. Once the glasses had been refilled, Mr. Malanion went on. "I suspect that you will soon have a new customer at your barbershop, Mr. Moses. Are those not the beginnings of whiskers sprouting on Ted's chin?"

"Aye," said my father. "I believe you are right, Mr. Malanion. I have noticed the same thing myself."

"Pa!" I said.

"That will be a good thing, will it not Doctor?" asked Ma. "Now that Theodore is almost a man of medicine, it seems fitting that he look more mature. A beard will add dignity and make him appear older than his years."

"Ma! Please!"

"I agree," said J.B. "Patients prefer proclaiming their pains to an older man. Beards breed confidence."

"J.B.!"

Doctor Wilkinson pretended he did not hear me and squinted across the table to inspect my chin. "Now that Ted is a godfather, it seems appropriate that he appear more dignified. Yes, I think you should let your whisker—excuse me, whiskers—continue to grow, Ted."

"I do not have whiskers," I said, too loudly, "and it is no one's concern if I do." I reached across the table for the bottle of cordial, but Ma was faster than I, and whisked it out of my grasp.

"You may be fourteen, young man, but one small glass to celebrate your birthday is all you may have. No more cordial for you."

My father surprised everyone, especially me, by taking the bottle from Ma. "He is nearly a grown man, Jeannie. A small second glass will not hurt him."

"Indeed it will not," said J.B. "Mrs. MacIntosh's chokecherry cordial is well known for its curative properties. It stimulates the mind and cleanses the blood. I believe that I, too, would indulge in another glass, with your permission, Mrs. MacIntosh. I spent a restless—no, actually a sleepless—night and am in need of a small stimulant."

"You do look tired, Doctor, and you may certainly have another glass, if you will explain what you meant about Ted being a godfather."

"Ah," said J.B., pouring himself a substantial portion of cordial, "your son has neglected to tell you about his new role in life, has he? Ted, you have been remiss. Shall I explain?"

He did explain about Mrs. Fraser and the twins, and managed to make it sound quite logical that the babies be named Robert and Andrew instead of being named for their godfathers. I was glad to let him do the talking, and Ma was more than happy that there would be infants in her life once again. She began making plans to visit the new parents, discussing what I should buy as a gift for my godchild.

After the meal, Mr. Malanion and I played our violins while Pa whirled my mother around the room in a short but vigorous dance. I watched, surprised. I had no idea that my father knew how to handle himself on a dance floor. Ma was panting slightly and fanning herself when the music ended.

J.B. danced with Ma, too, and then she took the violin from my hand and pulled me to the centre of the floor. I had never danced before, and I felt uncomfortable. But when Mr. Malanion ended the piece and I bowed to my mother and escorted her back to her seat there was much applause and laughter. I think I did rather well.

J.B., however, did not join in the laughter. He looked paler than he had earlier, and now deep lines creased his face.

"My thanks for the meal, Mrs. MacIntosh, but I regret that I must leave," he said abruptly. "Be at the surgery early in the morning, Ted. We have much to do." Then he was gone, the front door shutting firmly behind him.

My parents looked at each other. "Should we go with him?" asked my mother. "Do you think ...?"

"I do not know, Jeannie," my father answered, but it was Moses who rose to his feet.

"I, too, shall take my leave," he said. "Perhaps I can catch up to the doctor before he reaches town. I saw the pain in his face as he watched the dancing. He was remembering happier times."

"If you think it necessary, Mr. Moses," said my mother, escorting Moses to the door. "But I can not believe that Doctor Wilkinson's problem has returned. He gave me his word that it would not."

Moses spoke to her softly, but I heard him anyway. "Such trouble as the good doctor has known can not always be ended by words," he said before he hurried out.

Mr. Malanion played a few more tunes, but the brightness had gone from the party. Then he, too, bid us farewell and left.

The cheerful evening had ended much differently than it had begun. I was disgruntled again, and puzzled. Why had J.B. left so suddenly? I helped Ma with the washing up, but neither of us spoke much and the kitchen was nearly silent as we worked.

When the last glass was dry and all the good dishes carefully stored in the sideboard, Pa called me and I went into the front room.

"Here," he said, taking a small velvet bag from his pocket and handing it to me. "It was your great-grandfather's. He would wish you to have it, since you are his namesake."

Inside the bag was the gold pocket watch which my father wore only on Sundays. I held it in my hand for a moment, feeling the smoothness of it, then lifted it to my ear. Pa smiled at me.

"You used to do that in church when you were small," he said. "Many a time the ticking of that watch soothed your restlessness or stilled your cries. I thought that you would have more use of it than I; a doctor's assistant has need of a reliable timepiece."

"Thank you, Pa," I said, and turned the watch over to look at what was engraved on the back. *P. MacIntosh.* 'P' for Percival.

"Wear it in good health, son," said my father. "May it number many happy years for you."

"Many, many happy years," said my mother. "Happy birthday, Ted." I kissed her good night, but before I could escape to my room she stopped me.

"Ted, I think that you should stay home tomorrow," she said. "Doctor Wilkinson did not look well tonight. He most likely will rest and will not need your help."

"But J.B. told me to be early," I said. "If he is ill there will be even more for me to do. I may have to tend to some of the patients myself."

My voice got louder as I went on speaking. "I do not understand, Ma. J.B. told me to stay home today but you insisted I go. Now he tells me to come to work tomorrow, yet you tell me I should stay home. Will someone please explain what is happening?"

"Ian?" said my mother, not answering me but turning to my father.

My father did not answer me, either. "I have faith in Doctor Wilkinson, Jeannie," he said to my mother. "Let Ted go to work as usual. I think all will be well."

"I hope you are right, Ian," said my mother. "With all of my heart, I hope that you are right."

Eight

In spite of J.B.'s warning, I did not arrive for work early. Ma had neglected to tell either me or J.B. that she had arranged to have my photograph taken that morning. She had insisted I wear my good suit and had shown me how to attach my new watch to the watch chain, then tuck it into the small vest pocket.

The photographer had taken a long time arranging my pose. Finally he had sighed, "You have outgrown that suit, Ted. The sleeves are far too short. Put one arm behind you. Perhaps it won't be so obvious."

When I finally got to J.B.'s surgery, he said, "I told you to be prompt this morning. It is now much past the time I expected you."

"I'm sorry, J.B."

"Perhaps then you will honour me with your presence longer than usual tonight. There is a shipment of pharmaceuticals at Barnard's Express which has arrived and needs to be fetched, colic medicine to be mixed for the twins who have spent an uncomfortable night and turpentine salve to be prepared, among other chores. I have left you a list of what you are to do today. See to it that everything is finished before you leave."

He sat down at his desk and pulled open a book, paying no more attention to me. I went into the dispensary, blinking in surprise when I saw the room. The bed was unmade, the blankets badly twisted and tangled together. J.B.'s clothes were heaped on the floor, almost as if they had fallen from their hooks at once or as if someone had thrown them down. Several cups lay in puddles of stale coffee on the table, a plate had dried food crusted on it, and there was a broken bowl on the floor. J.B. was not a neat person, but today the dispensary was unusually dishevelled. I didn't think I had seen it in this disreputable a condition since my first day as his apprentice.

There was nothing to do but to begin cleaning up, for I could not attend to any of the medical chores with the dispensary in this state. I lit a fire and went for water. While it heated so I could clean the dishes, I would make the bed and tend to his clothes.

I wanted to show J.B. my new watch. We should have a laugh over the initial of my middle name engraved on it, I thought. However, it did not seem like the best time to approach him, not in his present mood. I pulled the watch out to look at it, then put it away again. If I listened hard, I could hear it ticking, even tucked away in my pocket. I took it out, then put it away, then took it out again. There was a comfort in the solid feel of the watch and I liked the way the rich gold of its case caught the light. Whenever I turned it over and saw the engraving, I smiled to myself. This watch had always kept perfect time, but just to make sure I would step into the surgery and compare it with the clock J.B. kept on his desk.

He looked up as I came into the room and frowned at me. "Is that, by any chance, a new watch you have?"

"It was my great-grandfather's," I said, eager to show it to him. "Then it was my grandfather's, then my father had it, and now he has given it to me. Here, look at the name on the back."

"I do not care what may be engraved on it. I only care that the work I assigned you be completed. However, since you neglected to close the dispensary door behind you, I have been able to see that you check the passage of time regularly. Perhaps returning your new timepiece to your pocket and leaving it there for, oh, maybe ten minutes at once, would free your hands to continue your chores."

He turned his back on me and returned to his reading. I swallowed hard, slipped the watch back into my pocket and hoped that J.B.'s ill temper would soon pass. I could not remember him ever being so sharp tongued.

After I finished tidying and cleaning the dispensary, I checked the list to see what I should tackle next. There was laudanum to be prepared, licorice root to be ground and mixed into a tonic, and several other mixtures to be made ready with their dosage instructions written out. I would leave the preparation of the salve until last because the fumes from the turpentine sometimes made me feel ill. I went to the chest which held the medicinal ingredients to fetch the opium I needed for the laudanum. Drops of liquid opium had to be counted very carefully according to the doctor's instructions. The drops were added to a sweet tasting liquid to try to cover the bitter taste, although patients who took laudanum regularly claimed that they no longer noticed the bitterness.

The lid to the chest stood open, so I did not have to ask J.B. for the key. That relieved me. The fewer things I had to ask him today, the fewer times I should be subjected to his surly mood. However, when I picked up the bottle of opium, I saw that it was nearly empty. I thought that there had been more, but perhaps J.B. had dispensed some without my knowledge. There was another bottle in the order J.B. had said had arrived, but I would have to go to the express office and fetch the supplies before I could begin this task. It seemed that every order J.B. placed lately contained liquid opium, I thought. We were using a lot of it these days.

The chest which held the medical supplies had drawers in the sides of it, but when you opened the lid you saw the entire space at the top of the trunk was filled with a wooden shelf containing small partitions. The bottles and jars of ingredients fit snugly into these wooden compartments, each one labelled and in its own space. This trunk had belonged to a ship's medical officer, J.B. had explained, which was why everything was so securely held in place. That was necessary so that when the ship sailed through rough weather, the bottles and jars did not roll about and smash into each other.

As I let the lid of the chest drop closed something shattered, and when I looked I saw that a bottle had broken. It had contained flowers of sulphur, a bright yellow powder. That container must have been incorrectly placed in its compartment so that it stood too high. I looked, dismayed, at the fine powder which now was scattered over the entire contents of the chest.

"Too much merriment last night," said J.B. He was standing in the doorway between his surgery and the back room, and he glared at me. "If my assistant is to be so clumsy after every celebration, I shall soon be deeply in debt replacing what he breaks and destroys."

"I'm sorry, J.B., but the bottle was not properly replaced. It was not my fault—"

"Oh, it is my fault, then? I am the one who was careless with my medicines, am I? How dare you say that to me!"

I looked at him, startled. His eyes were red and his hands shook slightly as he leaned against the door frame, glaring at me. His skin had an unhealthy look to it; it was sallow and gleamed with sweat.

"Are you unwell, J.B.? Can I be of assistance?"

"I am not unwell and it is no concern of yours. You have much to do today. Do it. I am leaving." He picked up his black doctor's bag, jammed a hat on his head and left, slamming the door behind him.

"J.B.?" I started to go after him, but then changed my mind. His foul temper this morning surely had nothing to do with me. Perhaps he had been with patients most of the night and needed sleep and that was why he was so irritable and ill looking. He had been tired at my birthday party, but now he looked far worse than he had then.

Shrugging my shoulders, trying to shake off J.B.'s hurtful words, I checked the list of his instructions once more and set to work.

I didn't see him again that day. Patients arrived during scheduled surgery hours, and I had to send them away. I dispensed the medicines J.B. had asked me to prepare, but I could do nothing for most of those who wished to see the doctor.

"He is attending someone else," I said, not knowing if I spoke the truth. "Come back later."

A few of his patients returned, but J.B. did not. Where was he? It was unusual for him not to tell me where he was going. He never left me alone in the surgery without giving me instructions about what to do for any patients he expected.

I spent some time trying to clean up the yellow sulphur powder which lay over everything in the medicine chest, but soon gave up. The fine powder had drifted everywhere, coating the contents of the chest and settling into every corner and crevice. I removed bottles and wiped them, but as soon as I replaced them in their compartments, they acquired another film of yellow dust, stirred up by my movements.

I did what I could. In the late afternoon, when J.B. still had not returned, I picked up the order from Barnard's Express, then took the colic medicine to Mrs. Fraser. I spent a long time with her and the twins, trying to help her as she gave them the mixture. That chore turned out to be more difficult than I would have thought. The babies were small, but they squirmed and wriggled and it was almost impossible to get the mixture into them. We finally succeeded, but I thought that I would add more sugar when I mixed their colic medicine again. Perhaps they did not care for the taste.

"This will help a great deal," I told Mrs. Fraser, trying to sound confident. "The doctor will be back soon, but for tonight I know this medicine will give all of you a better rest." To myself, I added, "I sincerely hope I'm right."

But J.B. had not come back when, late in the day, I left the surgery and went home. I was too worried to eat much at dinner, and when I finally slept I dreamt of J.B. He was calling to me, but when I went to search for him, he was not there. Although that dream could hardly have been called a nightmare, it left me uneasy the next morning. Uneasy, and worried.

My mother sensed my mood, and asked if I was feeling poorly.

"No. I am well."

"And Doctor Wilkinson?" she asked. "He is no longer so fatigued?"

"He is well, too," I said, and changed the subject. I did not want to tell her of J.B.'s strange behaviour. Surely today he would be back to attend to his patients and I would not have to make excuses for his absence over and over again.

The door to the surgery was unlocked, and when I pushed it open I saw that J.B. *had* returned. He was sitting at his desk, sprawling across it, his head resting on the desk top and one arm dangling beside his chair.

"J.B." I said, going to him. "I am relieved that you are back."

He did not answer me. I put my hand on his shoulder and shook it, gently. "Are you asleep?"

Still there was no answer. I shook him once again. "J.B., wake up."

He groaned and lifted his head from the desktop. Today he looked even worse that he had yesterday. His skin was not just sallow, it was almost white with a waxy sheen. He had not shaved, and the bristles of his beard showed black against his paleness. His eyes were red-rimmed and watery, and it seemed he kept them open with great difficulty.

"Who are you?" he asked, peering at me, puzzled.

"Who am I?" I was too surprised to think of anything else to say.

The doctor blinked and stared harder. "Of course. You are Ted MacIntosh. Forgive me, my mind seems confused today. Well, how can I help you?"

"J.B., I ..." was all I could manage. "I ... I mean ..."

He tried to straighten up in his chair, and rubbed his hands across his face before speaking again. "You mean what? Quickly, young sir. I have important things on my mind. What are you doing here, what do you want of me?"

"I am your assistant. Don't you remember?"

"Assistant. I could use one of those. Fine, consider yourself hired. Now leave me alone." He put his head back on his desk, cradling it in his arms.

"J.B.? What is wrong? Surely you can not have forgotten that I have been your assistant for many weeks. You must be ill."

His voice when he answered was indistinct. He did not raise his head, and the words were muffled. "I remember, please forgive me. I am not ill, but I can not sleep, Ted. I can not sleep."

Relief filled me. His memory was not gone; he would be all right. I spoke cheerfully. "No, you most certainly can not sleep now, J.B. You have patients who will begin to arrive shortly, having missed you yesterday. There will be many of them and some will be angry at you, I am afraid."

He lifted his head and smiled at me. At least, I think he believed it was a smile. It looked more like a grimace.

"No, you misunderstand. I do not mean that I can not sleep now, at this moment. At night, all night. I have not slept since Mrs. Fraser's twins were born. I am sick for lack of a night's rest."

"Do you dream, J.B.? Is it nightmares which keep you awake, dreams of Mrs. Cameron and her children?"

"I can not find sleep, Ted, not anywhere, not at all. My eyes close, but my mind will not stay still. It jumps and twitches and ties itself into great knots of anguish."

"I don't understand," I said.

"No, I had not thought you would." Again his face twisted into that horrible spasm as he tried once more to smile. "Dreams, ah, the dreams, Ted, the dreams. Those which come at night, that are brought by sleep, those are unwelcome. Dreams that come during the daylight, those are much, much better. I fear I have dreamt too much during the day, and sleep has forsaken me at night."

His eyes slid away from me and, mumbling something I could not understand, he lowered his head and stared intently at a large stain on the desk top. It was dried ink, and it had not been there when I left the surgery last night. J.B. picked up an uncorked ink bottle lying on its side, frowned, then began to rub his fingers across the stain. "A stain, a spot," he said. "A wretched spot."

Suddenly he lifted his head and threw the empty ink bottle at me. I ducked and J.B. laughed. "Out, out damned spot," he said. "Out, out damned Ted."

"What?"

"Get out. Go. Leave. Dispatch yourself. Depart. Depart directly."

"J.B.? Why do you want me to leave? I don't understand. Let me get Doctor Bell for you ..."

"What Doctor Bell, which Doctor Bell, wherefore Doctor Bell? Nevermore Doctor Bell. What, bring in a physician to watch me while I wrestle with slumber? Never. The Bell shall not toll for me. Especially not belligerent Doctor Bell. Go away, Ted. Leave me. Now."

He spoke like a madman. Perhaps he had contracted brain fever, perhaps some other disease which made him act this way. I must get help for him, but I was afraid to go to fetch a physician. Once I left the surgery, I felt sure that J.B. would lock the door and refuse to let me, or anyone else, enter. I could not leave him, but I didn't know what to do if I stayed.

J.B. had prescribed laudanum to help me sleep when my nightmares were so troublesome. Why did he not take laudanum or a similar medicine himself? There was none prepared, but I could mix some and offer it to him. Once he slept, perhaps his mind would clear. Lack of sleep can make anyone irrational and ill.

My mind was made up. I would go to the dispensary and mix a mild tincture of laudanum and make sure that J.B. took it. There was more than enough opium to prepare the mixture; there had been a full bottle in the order I picked up from the express office yesterday.

I would get J.B. to bed, make him drink some warm tea, give him the medication, and stay to watch over him. I would have to explain to his patients that he was unavailable, but there were other doctors in Barkerville who could tend to any emergencies until he had recovered.

J.B. could not see patients in this state, and I did not intend to let any of them get even a small glimpse of him. He looked so ill and his manner was so peculiar that he would surely frighten them. They might never again trust him as a physician.

He was silent now. With his head down on his arms he could not see me, and if I were quiet he would not know that I had not left as he had ordered me to.

Cautiously, trying not to make a sound as I moved, I went to the dispensary and eased the door shut behind me. I straightened the doctor's bed, lit the stove and set a kettle of water on to boil. Then I went to the medicine chest to gather up the ingredients to prepare laudanum.

Again today the lid to the chest stood open, and I could see that some of the containers had been replaced incorrectly. I moved things around, setting them right, then pulled the bottle of opium from the compartment where it was kept. There was a smell in the chest, too, a strong smell. It wasn't just the sulphur I had spilled yesterday, it was another medicine as well.

Something was wrong. I had put the new bottle of opium in here after picking up the order from Barnard's Express. When I had prepared laudanum for a patient yesterday, I had used up what was left in the old bottle and taken only a few drops from the new supply. Now *that* bottle was almost empty.

I looked more closely into the chest, and I sniffed. Something else had been spilled, something with a bitter smell which almost overpowered the sulphur odour.

It was liquid opium. It had been spilled over the bottles and jars in the chest and had mixed with the sulphur powder which I had not been able to completely remove when I cleaned the chest. The liquid opium had dried stickily, combining with the sulphur to form yellow clumps. It looked as if small gold nuggets were sprinkled across the contents of the medicine chest.

I suddenly felt frightened. J.B. moaned and sat up, looking wildly around him, then collapsed back onto his desk, his head thumping as it fell. Jumping at the noise, I swallowed nervously and took a deep breath.

Then I ran for my father.

Nine

Once before I had run to my Pa's carpentry shop as frightened as I was now, but *then* I had collided with James Barry. This time no one would stop me. I burst in the door and barely paused to take a breath.

"Pa," I gasped. "Oh, Pa. I don't know what to do."

He took one look at me and put down the table leg he was sanding. "Is it the doctor, son?"

"Yes. Something is wrong with him."

"I am not surprised. I thought he looked frail at your birthday celebration."

"I don't know what has happened," I said. "He looks terrible and he won't stand up and when he talks it makes no sense at all. It's frightening."

My father nodded. "No need to be frightened, son. In my opinion, Doctor Wilkinson's conversation makes little sense even when he is *not* ill. But I will come with you and see what is wrong. I suspect that his trouble has returned to plague him again."

"What trouble? I don't understand. What's wrong with him?"

My father took his pot of glue off the stove, then pulled his apron over his head and hung it up. "The opium, son. Some years ago, Doctor Wilkinson began to take too much of his own medicine. It became a habit, and it was only with great difficulty and the help of his friends that he overcame the addiction."

"Opium? J.B. is not ill or in pain. He has no *reason* to take opium."

"Not ill," said my father, ushering me out the door and closing it behind him. "Not in the body. But there was much pain in his heart when Sophia Cameron died. At first the opium eased his agony, but then it became his greater torment. I am sorry to hear he has succumbed again, but this time we will deal with him quickly before the drug has him too firmly in its grasp."

My father took one look at J.B. and told me to fetch Doctor Bell. Then I was firmly sent away. J.B. would be taken care of, I was told. I was not needed. Feeling extremely disgruntled, I went home.

෴

And at home I stayed. Except for trips to town to visit with Moses, to fetch supplies for my mother, or to borrow books from the library, I did not leave my house for almost two weeks.

I heard nothing about J.B. When I asked about him, my father only said that Doctor Wilkinson was being well taken care of, but was not able to receive visitors.

"I am not a visitor," I said one day as Pa and I worked together in Ma's garden. "I'm his assistant. And his friend."

"Nevertheless, Ted, you would not be welcome. Give the doctor a while longer to recover. Once he is more himself, he will be glad to see you, but not yet. He needs time to regain his health and his sensibilities."

"He will want to see *me*," I said. "Is he in the hospital?"

"No, son. But he is being well taken—"

"I know, you keep saying that. But what is wrong with him? Why did he make himself so ill?"

My father straightened up and wiped the sweat from his face. He leaned on the hoe he had been using around the hills of potatoes, and looked at me seriously.

"Perhaps it *is* time we told you the rest of the story son. Then you will better understand what has happened to your friend."

"I *knew* that J.B. had not told me everything! There's more about Mrs. Cameron isn't there?"

"Aye, but also about the doctor."

"Tell me, Pa." I had been kneeling in the soft dirt, but I stood up and faced him.

"Before Mrs. Cameron died, she told her husband she did not want to spend all of eternity here in the goldfields. She called it a hateful place and made him promise to take her home, to be buried with her own people."

"Home?"

"Ontario. On December 22, exactly two months from the day his wife died, Cariboo's claim paid off. He was now a very rich man, so he had a special coffin built for Sophia. It was solid, lined with tin, and watertight. He filled it with whiskey before placing her in it."

"*Whiskey?* In her *coffin?*"

"Mrs. Cameron had a long journey ahead of her, Ted. Although she left Barkerville in the dead of winter, her trip would take her much further south, where it was warmer. As a doctor's apprentice you surely must have learned that alcohol, any type of alcohol, is an excellent preservative."

"It is," I agreed, swallowing hard.

"Mr. Cameron hired men to help him carry his wife," my father went on. "The gossips have said that he also took with him a fifty pound sack of gold, but I do not know the truth of that. I do know he paid the men well—twelve dollars a day with a two thousand dollar bonus when they reached Victoria."

"That is a great deal of money!"

"It was well earned, son. The snow was so deep that pack horses could not be used for much of the journey and the men had to carry Mrs. Cameron on their backs. I have heard it said that they often lost their footing on the frozen trail, and that her coffin fell many times. She suffered dreadfully."

"She was dead. She didn't suffer."

"Maybe not, but those who went with her did. So many miles to travel with only a dead wife and her grieving husband for company."

"Did they reach Victoria, Pa?"

"That they did, and in the spring of 1863, Mrs. Cameron was buried there, awaiting passage on a ship to take her and Cariboo to Ontario. Finally she arrived home and was buried once more in the family graveyard."

"She was buried three times?"

"Each time with a proper service, so they say. Also—"

"The boy has heard enough," my mother said. I did not

know how long she had been listening, but her voice was angry.

"There is no need for him to know everything, Ian. It is ghoulish to be speaking of such things."

"But, Ma—"

"I said you have heard quite enough, Theodore. Doctor Wilkinson is your friend. Why would you wish to pry into his life in this way? I can not understand why your father would repeat such gossip. Ted, you will finish the weeding alone. Ian, I would have a word with you. Right now."

I watched my father as he slowly followed my mother into the house and I thought I was very happy to stay outside with the chickweed and the dandelions.

In the next two weeks I chopped enough firewood for the entire winter. I split kindling and I cleared bush from around Ma's garden, pulling fiercely at every weed I found. Pa requested my help digging a new hole for the backhouse and the two of us spent most of the day labouring with our shovels and then gently edging the small building into its new position. It was all hard work, but none of it helped me forget.

I missed J.B., missed his laugh, even missed the way he played with words. "I most miserably miss you, J.B." I said to myself. "Please promise to promptly recover. Please come back."

Still no one spoke of J.B. at all. His condition, like his location, was a secret, at least from me. "He is well taken care of. He is mending," was all I could get out of anyone. It seemed that there was a conspiracy among the town's adults not to mention him. Pa would not talk to me again about Mrs. Cameron or about J.B. no matter how many times I asked him.

I who had spent weeks as J.B.'s closest companion, who knew of his nightmares and his fears, who had helped him scrub his dispensary and deliver the twins, was not allowed to share in the secret.

For almost a month I stayed close to home, chopping firewood, assisting Ma with her chores, sometimes reading from one of the medical books that J.B. had loaned me. But without J.B. to help me with the words I didn't understand or to explain the Latin names for the diseases, reading soon became boring.

My father suggested more than once that I return to work with him in the carpentry shop, and one day I did. I brought home a small piece of sanded wood, thinking I would spend some time whittling and carving. I sat in the sun with my knife, but at the end of two hours what had taken shape beneath my hands was not the book-end I had intended, but a distorted face, its mouth open in a scream. I threw it into the fire and did not return to Pa's shop.

Even Moses, whom I visited frequently these days, would not tell me anything. I strained my ears when he chatted to his customers, hoping that someone would pass on a bit of information about J.B. But either no one knew or no one would speak while I was present.

On the door of the doctor's locked surgery was a "Closed" sign, and the curtains had been drawn tightly. The building looked so deserted that I usually turned my eyes away from it when I walked by; its emptiness made me sad. But one day I stopped and stared at the surgery door, realizing that I felt anger as much as sadness.

I was angry at J.B., angry at my parents and the other adults who spoke only in whispers, angry at being ignored, angry because J.B. did not want to see me, angry because I was lonely.

There was no one on the street near me, so I picked up a big piece of dried mud and hurled it at the surgery door. It hit the "Closed" sign and shattered, scattering dust and pieces of dirt across the front step. Then I turned my back on Doctor Wilkinson's empty surgery and walked away, vowing never to look at it again.

One morning late in June, Ma sent me to town to do some shopping. She had been doing that a lot recently, finding something for me to attend to in Barkerville nearly every day. Since many of her errands were not all necessary ones, I think she just wanted to get me out from under her feet. I didn't really want to go anywhere, but I dared not argue with Ma. She had that look on her face again, a look that had been there frequently since I had been at home.

In spite of my vow, I still glanced at the surgery each time I passed it and I did so again today, flicking my eyes away almost immediately. Then I looked a second time. The door was open, wide open, as were the curtains. The "Closed" sign had gone and someone had swept away the clumps of dirt from the front step. I hesitated, unsure whether to continue on to Mason and Daly's store or whether to go to the surgery and see if maybe ...

"Good morning, Ted. I need your help most desperately. In my absence, the dust has grown thick and the mice have made meals of many of my books. Come on, lad. To work. To work." The doctor called to me from the doorway, smiling, his smile as wide and as happy as it had ever been.

"J.B.? You are back? You are well?"

"As well as ever I was, Ted, and perhaps even better. My enforced rest has done me good but, ah, it was a difficult time. Doctor Bell is a demanding physician, and I believe that I have recovered in spite of myself purely to get away from his ministrations. Yes, I am back. It is good to see you, Ted."

"Welcome, J.B. I have missed you a great deal."

"You mean that you have been moping miserably while I malingered? Well, I malinger no more."

Ma's errands could wait. I stepped eagerly into the surgery. J.B. reached out his hand to clasp mine then, the handshake forgotten, put his arms around me in a warm embrace.

"It does my heart good to see you, my friend. It is a pleasure to see anyone who is not a product of my own twisted nightmares and hallucinations. But it is especially good to see *you*."

He released me from the bear-hug, clapping me on the shoulder and smiling broadly.

"Are you sure you are recovered?" I asked. Although J.B. smiled I could see that there were tears in his eyes and I was not at all sure that he was completely well.

"Yes, I have mended. I am well. I have returned from another journey and although it was a difficult one, I am back."

"You have been away on a trip?" I asked. "I did not know

you had been away."

"No, my body stayed in one place. Only my mind travelled, taking over and over again every step of that journey with Sophia Cameron."

"With Mrs. Cameron? You mean, you ... you went with Cariboo Cameron when ..."

"Yes, I thought you knew."

No, I hadn't known, not until now. This was the rest of the story, the part my mother would not let Pa tell me. J.B. had been one of the men who carried Mrs. Cameron's body away from the goldfields.

"I didn't know," I said. "It ... it must have been very difficult for you."

"It was, Ted. Sometimes I still feel the weight of her coffin." J.B. reached up and rubbed at his left shoulder as if it were tender. He realized what he was doing, put his arm down and smiled at me, but the smile quivered around the edges.

"She rested on my shoulders, Ted, but it is my heart which still pains me. At times it is too much for me to bear—the weight and the dreams. Can you understand that?"

I understood very well. I now knew that J.B. had earned his nightmares, as much as I had earned mine.

Ten

July came, and with it the thick heat of summer as well as blackflies, horseflies, houseflies, deer flies, gnats, and wasps. J.B treated heatstroke, rashes, broken legs, and sprained ankles. Patients complained of the heat, complained of the dust, complained about everything, although none of the complaints were very serious. J.B. listened a lot, offered much advice and recommended spruce tea for almost every ailment. I brewed spruce tea by the kettleful, improving on the doctor's recipe with a bit of sugar and a few drops of oil of peppermint, and J.B. claimed that his patients were thriving on the tonic. He told me that I had the instincts of a great healer, so I did more reading in medical books and decided that perhaps oil of cloves and a touch of anise would help the taste and the effectiveness of the colic medicine the twins consumed regularly. Both anise seed and cloves were frequently recommended for improving digestion. Mrs. Fraser claimed that my new mixture gave the babies much relief, and I proudly wrote the recipe down for J.B., adding it to his files.

That summer there was also a great demand for salve to relieve insect bites and sunburns, but I could not find a better substitute for the turpentine which J.B. insisted I use. Camphor was less strong smelling, but it did not offer the same relief, according to our patients. I also grew adept at concocting smelling salts which my mother said were the most effective she had ever used. Women were very prone to fainting in the summer, as they worked long hours over hot stoves, canning vegetables, meat, and fish for the winter, and boiling fruits for jellies and preserves.

J.B. taught me how to apply a mustard plaster for the lingering summer coughs and chest congestion which afflicted many in the goldfields, and once I successfully tended to a bloody finger (without the slightest bit of light-headedness) while J.B. was busy with another patient. I continued to read, to learn, to keep busy. Life in the doctor's surgery was much the same, but yet it was much, much different. For one thing, J.B. no longer stocked opium, no longer prescribed it, and I no longer prepared laudanum.

"There are other physicians who will give you that drug, if you feel you must have it," I heard him say, over and over to his patients. "I have no wish to have opium nor any of its relatives under my roof ever again. It will prove a false friend, no matter how much you believe it will relieve your pain." Some patients switched to other doctors, but many did not. Oddly, those that needed relief from pain claimed that they did just as well with an infusion of willow bark which J.B. now had me concocting and which he dispensed freely. It was another recipe he had learned from a Shuswap wise-man or shaman, and we were both pleased with how effective it was.

All that summer, with the sun rising early and not setting before ten in the evening, I worked at J.B.'s side. Yet never once did he speak to me about his long absence, never did he tell me where he had been or who, besides Doctor Bell, had cared for him during his illness. He also never spoke of how he had suffered. But I knew that he had suffered and I could see that he had changed. It wasn't only his refusal to keep opium in his medicinal supplies, it was a quietness which he carried about him, a stillness, as if he were listening to soft, distant voices. He still laughed, but less often, and his smile carried a sadness in it which had not been there before he became ill. He was there with me, yet he was not. He was absent-minded and, although never short-tempered, he spoke less and made fewer jokes. I worried about him, fearing that some part of him still was ill, that perhaps he would never again be whole.

I only left his side to go home to bed. All through the month of July, through the heat and through the week of torrential rains which brought cooler nights and also a new crop of mosquitoes, I stayed as close to J.B. as I could. When he went on a house call, I accompanied him, whether he wished me to or not. I took my noon meal with him, and also my evening meal, leaving the surgery only when he insisted. I arrived early in the morning, usually before he was awake, and made sure there was hot coffee ready when he arose.

"You have become one of my guardian angels, Ted," he said once. Then he smiled. "But you do not need to hover so."

"I am not 'hovering,'" I said, indignantly. "I am only trying to be of as much help as possible and to ..."

"To keep me safe from myself as well, I assume. You are doing a grand job of that, Ted. I have scarcely had a moment alone since I returned from ... since I recovered from my trouble. For that I thank you."

"No need to give me thanks."

"But I do thank you, my friend. However, I would appreciate it if tonight you could return home to eat as I have an appointment to meet Bridget for a meal and later to go dancing."

"Bridget? From the Hotel de France? The one who helped you deliver the twins?"

"Yes. She is also one of my guardian angels. She has taken me under her wing and makes sure that I am not alone at night—well, some nights, anyway."

"She stays here all *night*?"

"No, Ted, that would not be proper and you know it. But I often visit her. Bridget cared for me in her home while I was ill and ..."

"Bridget? You were with her? The whole time?"

"Yes. She nursed me through my black days, through the darkness—well, that is over. Now I would like to take her dancing. Guardian angels can also dance."

"I can stay with you if you are lonely. There is no need to go to her."

"Ted, I am very fond of you. I treasure our friendship and am grateful for the concern you have for my well-being. But you do not have graceful feet on the dance floor, nor do you make biscuits so light they melt in one's mouth."

"Why do your stomach and your feet mean so much to you?"

He smiled. "You will understand better in a few years. Between you and Bridget, I am lucky to have received both the best of care and the best of friendship, but tonight I wish to kick up my heels and dance. So do not get angry, but please go home. After all, I must not neglect my social responsibilities."

"Although you neglect your friends," I said. "Unless they happen to be female." I slammed the door on my way out. How could he prefer Bridget's companionship to mine? How could he have been at her house the whole time he was ill while I was not told where he was? Why did no one tell me anything?

J.B. was standing in the doorway of the surgery when I took a quick look back. He grinned and waved. I ignored him and continued on my way home, walking tall and hoping I looked dignified.

I probably didn't.

◉◉

J.B. continued to see Bridget most evenings and, after refusing the invitation several times, I went with him. He was right. She did make excellent biscuits and she was a good companion. After my first visit, I found that I enjoyed being with them both. There was always much laughter and J.B. was more like his old self after a visit with Bridget. I went back often. They seemed to welcome my company, but they would not yet allow me to go with them when they went dancing at one of the saloons. Bridget had promised to teach me to dance, once my mother gave her permission. However, I knew that it would be a long time yet before my mother would allow me to enter a saloon, so I didn't feel too disgruntled at being excluded.

Although the days stayed hot and dry the first frost arrived in early August, a mild one but sufficient to destroy my mother's flower bed and some of the less hardy garden crops. The cottonwood leaves began to edge into colour, losing the dusty green of the summer and the garden produce was ready to gather. My mother's potatoes did well, and she also had an unfortunately large turnip crop. I am not fond of turnips, and the thought of eating them regularly throughout the coming winter was not something I looked forward to.

August 8 was the anniversary of James Barry's death, but the day passed before I realized its significance. I seldom thought of him at all anymore, seldom rushed past the place on the road where his laugh had so frightened me. That part of my life was over. My nightmares had ended, as J.B. had said they would.

When September arrived it too was hot and dusty, but the nights grew much colder. The month reached the mid-point and the colours on the trees deepened; some leaves began to fall and even those that remained green had a dry sound to them as they rustled in the wind. People began abandoning the goldfields, heading for warmer climates in which to spend the winter. Some shops were closed, more would be closing soon, and nearly every stagecoach leaving Barkerville was full.

Moses usually went to Victoria for the coldest months, returning to Barkerville in the spring when the creeks began to thaw and the deep accumulation of snow had almost disappeared from between the buildings. He was already making preparations for his journey and looking forward to the time he would spend on the Pacific Coast. My family would not be leaving this year; we would stay and see the winter through, and hope it would not be a bad one.

September 16, a day no one in Barkerville would ever forget, dawned cold, colder than one would expect considering how hot and dry the weather had been for so many weeks. When I walked down the hill to go to work, the road was frozen. In the ruts left by the wagons and stagecoaches faint traces of ice nestled, and frost coated the bushes and grass beside the road. I was wearing my heavy winter jacket, but knew that well before noon it would be so warm that I would have removed the jacket and would be wishing that I did not have to work but could be out in the sunlight, enjoying the last days of summer.

Summer comes slowly here in the goldfields, but it always leaves in a hurry. From broiling heat and clouds of mosquitoes to frost on the grass tips and the crunch of frozen ground underfoot—the fall arrives overnight. I sighed, thinking of the long winter ahead and of the endless hours of dark which would come with it. All through the winter months, the sun would set in the late afternoon and not return until morning was half gone. I would grow tired of lamplight at both breakfast and the evening meal; tired of filling buckets with snow for Ma to melt so she could do the washing; tired of fighting through the night winds to bring in yet another load of wood for the stove.

Pulling my jacket tighter around me, I tried not to think of winter. It would arrive soon enough, whether I wished it to or not.

As I walked through Chinatown I saw that the water pipes, the flumes which carried water high across Barkerville's main street, were festooned with icicles. Overnight, as water had dripped through the joints which held the wooden pipes

Ann Walsh

together, it had frozen. The sun caught one of the flumes, Barker's flume as most called it, and the icicles gleamed as if they were polished silver. I stopped for a moment and stared, knowing that the sight would not last long. Last night there had been the Northern Lights, a display which was more spectacular than any I had ever seen, curtains of vivid colour waving across the sky for hours. This morning Jack Frost seemed to be trying to do his part to beautify the world.

A robin lit on Barker's flume and an icicle, jarred by the weight of the bird, fell to the ground. Other icicles would follow as the sun's heat grew stronger, and soon the flumes would be bare except for the constant dripping of water.

I took one last look at the glint of the sun on the icicles, and stepped inside J.B.'s surgery. "Good morning," I said. "And it is one, a very, very good morning. Have you seen the icicles on the water pipes?"

"I have seen both the frozen flumes and the flickering fireworks," said J.B. "I mean, of course, the Aurora Borealis which provided us with such spectacular entertainment last night. You, unfortunate lad, were not here, but the saloons emptied and people stood silently in the streets for hours, just watching."

"They left the saloons? I am sorry I missed that, J.B. It seems close to a miracle."

"It was, Ted, it was. For miners to abandon their beverages and stand shivering in the cold merely to pay homage to nature's display was indeed something near a miracle."

"I saw the Northern Lights, too," I said. "My parents and I watched for hours."

"Ah, then you were up past your usual time for bed and

116

would welcome a less strenuous day's work, would you not?"

"I'm fine. I wasn't that late, besides I don't need as much sleep anymore now that I'm—"

"Yes, yes, now that you're a grown man of fourteen."

"I only meant that now I sleep without nightmares, and so I sleep well. I was not referring to my age."

"Of course not. I apologize. However, I have a chore for you today—no, not a chore, rather a most important assignment—which will also allow you time to rest."

"I don't understand. Don't you need me in the dispensary? Have you no patient records which you wish me to update, no medications to prepare?"

"That will keep, Ted. I am not sure you will want to undertake this assignment, but I can not do it and someone needs to. Sit down and hear me out."

His words made me nervous. I moved a pile of books from a chair, replacing them on the shelves where they had been tidily stored when I left last night, and sat down, wondering why I felt so uneasy.

"Well? What is it you want me to do? Please, no jokes about me delivering babies. I did not find that amusing."

"No, Ted. No jokes. I want you to sit with a sick friend— well, an acquaintance, if not a close friend."

"One of our patients, J.B.?"

"No. Yan Quan is not a patient. He doctors himself in the way of his countrymen. But he is ill, very ill. Somehow he has upset the others of the Chinese community. No one will stay with him, no one will even speak his name aloud and no one will tell me what he did to make his friends so angry. Although they bring him food and medicine, he is left alone to die."

"To die?"

"I fear so. Already he has been taken to the Peace House, although I suspect he finds little peace there."

The Peace House. The tiny cabin behind the Tong building! I had never set foot inside that building, nor did I ever wish to.

"Well, Ted? There will be little for you to do—bring a book to read. Here, take the one on anatomy which you have been wanting to peruse. I am sure your mother will not mind, especially if she does not discover that you have been reading it."

J.B. rummaged on the other chair and found what he wanted. He handed the heavy book, *Anatomy of the Human Body*, to me, but I shook my head. I had long since taken a good look at the more interesting illustrations in that volume, without either J.B.'s or my mother's knowledge.

"Very well, then," said J.B. "Select other reading material to keep you occupied. Here, take my new reference book. It has just been published, after a thorough revision, and I received it not two days ago. This invaluable little volume is full of the latest information, everything a modern man of medicine needs to know. A truly comprehensive manual; one I could not do without. Here. See for yourself."

He proudly handed me a thick book, pocket sized, titled *The Physician's Vade Mecum.*

"What does 'Vade Mecum' mean?" I asked, taking the book. "Is it Latin?"

"Yes. The title literally means 'go with me' and this book, or one of its brothers, can be found in nearly every doctor's bag, a constant companion which has probably saved more lives than ... You have successfully changed the subject, Ted." He looked at me reproachfully and I squirmed, avoiding his eyes.

"What I ask will not be difficult," J.B. continued. "Just make sure Yan Quan is comfortable and give him water as he asks for it. He will take no medicines from me, but that is of little consequence now. I doubt that he will see tomorrow's sunrise."

"But, J.B., I ..."

"Have no fear, Ted. I will relieve you this afternoon, as soon as my last patient departs. I am sure that Yan Quan will not die before nightfall."

"I don't ... I mean ... do I have to do this?"

"If you care about your fellow man, Ted, and if you care about me, then you will do it. Is it so much to ask of one who aspires to be a physician himself in a few years? It will be an easy task for you, and Yan Quan will welcome your company as none of his countrymen will stay with him through this lonely time. Although I doubt he will speak much. His command of English is limited, and besides, he has other things on his mind than polite conversation."

"I really wanted to clean the dispensary today. It has been a while since the floor was well scrubbed and I notice that you have acquired a whole new collection of bottles which need to be washed and we need more salves prepared and ..."

J.B. sat down, pulling the other straight-backed chair close to mine. He had pushed the books piled on the chair to the floor, but no dust accompanied their arrival there. I had tended to the surgery, as well as the dispensary, recently and the floor was clean and dustless.

"I sense that something is seriously amiss," he said, putting one hand on my arm. "For such an able and competent assistant as you have shown yourself to be, I can not understand why you are balking at this simple task."

"I'm not ..." I began.

"Why are you so reluctant, Ted? You are pale, yet when you came in a few minutes ago your skin was flushed with enthusiasm. I, as a trained physician, have determined that you find my designated duty dreadfully disagreeable."

"Don't *do* that," I said. "With the words. Please."

"I will try to speak plainly. Now please tell me just as plainly, why you do not wish to sit with Yan Quan?"

How could I tell him? After all the time J.B. and I had been together, after we had shared our nightmares, after we had become such close friends—how could I tell him that I was afraid to go into the Peace House?

I could not tell him, so I muttered something about having had a late night and little sleep. Then I picked up the new book J.B. was so proud of, listened carefully to his instructions and, very reluctantly, left to go to where a man was dying.

Eleven

It was dark inside the Peace House, so dark that at first I could not see the man who lay on a narrow bed against the far wall. Tai Ping Fong was what the Chinese called this place, but it was only a small cabin, barely big enough to hold a bed, a wood cook stove and one chair pushed up to a rickety table. A single window was covered with dark cloth, and when I pulled the door closed behind me there was no light at all except that filtering through narrow gaps between the logs of the walls.

I decided to leave the door partly open and taking a deep breath, hoping to fill my lungs, if not my whole body, with courage, I stepped further into the cabin. The figure on the bed coughed, a thin, rasping sound, and I wondered if the breeze from the open door had made him uncomfortable. Perhaps I should keep the door shut, but it was so dark in here. There was an oil lamp on the table so I lit it, adjusted the wick, then reluctantly pulled the door closed.

The sick man moaned, and I went to him. His face was deeply creased, whether with pain or age I could not tell, and his eyes barely flickered open before he closed them again.

"I am Doctor Wilkinson's assistant, Mr. Quan. He sent me to stay with you. Can I do anything for you? Do you wish some water?"

"No." The word was spoken so softly that I could barely hear it.

"Mr. Quan?"

Once more his eyes flickered open, then closed. "No," he repeated, turning his face to the wall. His breath wheezed, and he moaned softly. Another wheeze, then a cough and then he was silent.

I pulled out the chair by the table and sat down. It was probably too dark to read; the lantern gave off only a feeble, smoky light. I looked longingly at the window, wondering if I could pull back the curtain and let at least a small amount of sunlight into the room, but then I thought of how Mr. Quan had turned his face away and wondered if light bothered him.

J.B. believed that Mr. Quan would not die until the night, and it was not yet noon. Nevertheless, I listened hard for the next breath from the still figure on the bed, and peered into the shadowy corners of the room as if I expected to see someone—or something—there.

There was nothing to fear, I told myself, nothing at all. After all, I had helped J.B. with other patients who were mortally ill. I had seen dying men before. Why should this be different? But it *was* much different from those other times. I could not seem to control myself; my whole body was trembling violently. Had I not been sitting, I think I would have fallen to the floor. What was wrong with me?

Another cough and deep breath from the bed, a word I could barely make out. "Cold."

Of course, I realized suddenly. The fire had gone out during the night, and the Peace House had become colder and colder. Even though the sun shone brightly today, its rays had not yet warmed this building; there would be no natural warmth in the Peace House until late afternoon. I wasn't shaking because I was afraid. I was cold!

Beside the stove was a bundle of kindling and some firewood, although not much. I lit the stove, but knew the fire would not burn long on the small supply of wood provided.

The fire caught easily, and soon the crackle of dry wood filled the room. A gust of wind brought a puff of smoke back down the chimney, and I adjusted the damper in the stovepipe, added more wood, then sat down again, not knowing what else to do.

In spite of the poor light, I opened the book I had brought with me and propped it against the lamp base. *The Physician's Vade Mecum: A Manual of the Principles and Practice of Physic* it said on the cover, a title which J.B. himself could have happily written. This was a new edition, an updated version of an older work. The revisions had been done by Doctor Guy and Doctor Harley, two famous physicians whose names even I had heard mentioned. Since J.B. had so heartily recommended the book, I opened it and began to read the introduction. *The first and most obvious requisite for a practitioner is to be able to recognize a disease when he sees it, to distinguish it from others that resemble it, and to foretell its probable course and termination.* That seemed rather obvious to me, so I skipped ahead.

Phthisis Pulmonalis or *Pulmonary Consumption* was the heading of one section, *Acute Pleurisy* was a few pages further on and *Gastritis* followed that. I wrestled with the pronunciation of *Epidermycosis Tonsurans*, wondering what on earth that was until I read further and found out that it was the formal name for ringworm of the scalp. My own head began to itch, so I abandoned that page. I was seriously considering whether to try to read the section (with illustrations) about *Amputation at the Hip-Joint* when the door swung open.

"Who is there?" I called out, leaping to my feet. The book fell to the floor with a crash and I gasped. Squinting against the sunlight which streamed into the room and left me almost blinded, I swallowed hard and asked again. "Is someone there?"

Sing Kee, the herbalist, came in, a basket of firewood hung over one arm, a tray balanced carefully in front of him.

"Hello, Master Ted. Doctor John told me you are in Tai Ping Fong with this sick man. This is good."

"Hello, Mr. Kee. Have you brought medicines?"

"Yes, also firewood, food, and water. You will be here all day? That is kind. His own people will not stay with him, but no man, not even a bad man, should die alone."

"What did Mr. Quan do that made everyone so angry at him?"

"I can not tell you. He dishonoured his country. No one will let his name pass their lips and his bones will stay here in this foreign land and never be sent back to his home in China. He has betrayed his friends and angered everyone. Even me, and I do not anger easily, Master Ted."

I looked over at the bed where it seemed that the still figure was breathing more quietly, almost as if he were listening to Sing Kee's words.

"I will not speak to him," Sing Kee said, gesturing with his head towards the bed, "but I will bring him medicine to help when his pain is great." He set the tray he carried on the table, pointing to a small glass bottle, hardly thicker than a pencil and about half as long. "A few drops in some warm tea when the pain makes him cry out," he said. "This will help the coughing and let him rest."

He picked up a teapot with a bound wicker handle and set it on the stove where it would stay warm. On the tray were two small cups (more like bowls as they had no handles) a tin jug and a larger bowl, covered with a cloth. "Here, in the jug, is fresh water, and there is food," said Sing Kee. "Rice, vegetables, meat. This man is too sick to eat, but you must. Drink the tea, too." He nodded goodbye, and turned to leave.

"Mr. Kee?" I called.

"Yes? What you need?"

I didn't need anything, but I didn't want him to go just yet. With the cheerful herbalist in the room, the Peace House seemed brighter and larger.

"Um ..." I said.

"Yes?" Mr. Kee asked again. "You have questions maybe? About the disease?"

"No. I mean, yes. Why is Mr. Quan dying?"

"Part illness, part demons. Your Doctor Wilkinson would say 'typhus', but I think this more than a disease of the body."

"Typhus. Typhoid Fever. Like Mountain Fever. I see."

Sing Kee nodded. "Me also. I see that you are not happy in the Tai Ping Fong. You wish me to stay with you, but I can not. Perhaps you think that spirits are here?"

"Oh, no, of course not. I do not believe in ghosts."

Sing Kee shook his head. "That is not a wise thing. The spirits of the dead will be angry if you deny them."

"I mean that I am not *afraid* of ghosts. Of spirits."

"Of course. And that is a wise thing. Spirits, like dogs, know when one is afraid. They are dangerous when they smell fear."

It was my turn to smile, wondering if I could wash away the scent of fear with coal-tar soap and a good scrubbing. "I definitely will not let any ghosts smell fear on me," I said. "It is just that I have never been in this place before, and ..."

"Most who die here have pure souls," said Sing Kee. "You have nothing to fear in Tai Ping Fong."

"I am not afraid," I said, too loudly. "I'm not. But I am alone and this is so different from my usual work."

"You will do well, Master Ted. You have a good soul and a gentle heart. The man here has need of goodness. He would thank you, if he could. Now, I must go back to my store. Try some tea. It will refresh you."

Sing Kee left. The door shut behind him, the sunlight no longer streamed across the cabin floor. The oil lamp flickered and I turned up the wick, wondering again if I dared pull the curtains from the window and let more light into the room. The fire crackled, but there was no need to add wood, already the cabin was stifling hot. I took off my jacket, checked to see that the patient slept comfortably, and settled down with *The Physician's Vade Mecum*, trying hard, in spite of the wavering lamplight, to concentrate on the small print.

Functions of the Nervous System ... Delirium ... Spectral Illusions ... Remarkable Delusions ... Mania ... Dreams ... The headings at the top of the pages blurred as I flipped through a section devoted to the workings of the mind. "Dreams," I said out loud. Perhaps I would take a closer look at what this book said about dreams and nightmares. I began to read.

Yan Quan cried out. The sound of his voice startled me, causing me to jump, jarring the table as I did so. The flame in the lamp flared up briefly then steadied.

Once more the sick man called out, but not in a language I could understand. What did he want, I wondered. What could I do for him? His voice was weak; it sounded like dry leaves rasping over frozen ground. Perhaps he was thirsty.

I poured water from the jug into a cup and took it to him, raising his head so he could drink. His lips were cracked and raw, and his hands, when he tried to lift them to steady the cup against his lips, were so thin they seemed almost the hands of a skeleton. I held the cup and Yan Quan sipped, then coughed. The cough racked his body; his head fell back against my hand and I watched helplessly as his chest convulsed and he fought to breathe. When he was finally still he was covered with sweat and his eyes were closed.

"Do you wish more water, Mr. Quan? Here ..." Again I offered him the cup.

His eyes fluttered open and he tried to shake his head, but the movement sent him into another spasm of coughing, fresh sweat beading across his face. I lowered him gently to the pillow.

"Mr. Quan? Are you all right?"

Even as I spoke I realized that of course Yan Quan wasn't all right. He was dying. It seemed that I could do nothing for him but ask him useless questions and try to give him water.

But what had Sing Kee told me to do? I was to put a few drops of the medicine he had brought into some warm tea. When the patient was in pain I was to administer it.

The tea in the pot on the stove had kept warm, almost too warm. I poured some, diluted it with water, then gently pulled out the tiny cork and added five drops from the slender vial to the cup. For a moment I thought I recognized the medicine by its smell, but I couldn't identify exactly what it was. It smelled strongly of unfamiliar herbs or spices, but also of something that was definitely familiar to me.

However, it didn't matter what Sing Kee's small bottle contained. I only hoped the medicine would do some good because Yan Quan's breathing had become more laboured. I went to the patient, raising his head once more, holding the cup to his lips. "This will help, Mr. Quan. Please, you must try to drink it."

He opened his eyes and looked directly at me for a long moment, but then his head fell to one side and his eyes closed again. I realized that he was too weak to stay upright. Knowing I could not hold him up and force the medicine down his throat, I made him as comfortable as I could on the pillow, then stood back, watching him and wondering what to do.

Should I fetch J.B.? He would know how to administer medicine to someone this ill. I set the cup back on the table, and went to the door. But what if Yan Quan died when I was away? What if he died alone because I went for help instead of staying in the Peace House as I had promised?

If I had a spoon, perhaps I could get the liquid into his mouth while he lay down so he would not have to raise his head or sit up in order to drink. But there were no spoons, no table utensils of any kind in the cabin. A quick search showed me nothing more useful than what was on the tray.

What could I do? In J.B.'s dispensary were glass droppers which I used when adding liquid ingredients to the medicines I mixed. A small dropper was what I needed, so I would go and get one. I had opened the door and even taken a step outside when I suddenly remembered how J.B. had taught Mrs. Fraser to give colic medicine to the twins when they were reluctant to accept it.

Taking one last regretful look at the sunlit street, I stepped back into the Peace House, closing the door behind me. I had no need to go running to J.B. for help. I knew what to do.

The cloth covering the dish of food Sing Kee had brought was clean. I tore a small strip from it, twisted the piece I had removed and dipped the end of it into the tea mixture. Then I sat close to Yan Quan and held the cloth over his lips, letting the mixture drip slowly into his mouth. Drop by drop it fell, and finally he swallowed. Again I moistened the piece of cloth and held it for him. The twins had sucked on the twisted cloth and taken their medicine that way, but this patient was too weak to do that. He barely had the strength to swallow, but he managed to take some of the mixture. Then, when less than half was gone, he fell asleep.

I wondered if I should try to wake him, encourage him to finish the tea and the medicine it contained, but then I realized that if he slept he was not in pain. It would be better to leave him, I thought. What he had managed to swallow of Sing Kee's medicine had done him good, and while he slept I would eat. Checking my watch, I saw that it was well past noon.

No wonder I was hungry.

There was still tea in the pot on the stove and I poured myself a cup, setting it beside the dish of food. The tea was strong and the flavour was slightly bitter, but it wasn't unpleasant. I sipped the tea and studied the dish of food. It smelled unfamiliar, different from any dish I had ever eaten, but I was hungry now, hungry enough to try anything. But how could I eat? There were no eating utensils in the cabin and only two thin, rounded pieces of wood, the length of a table knife on the tray.

I picked them up and awkwardly managed to get a few pieces of rice into my mouth. Then, looking around as if I expected my mother to appear and chastise me, I put them down and ate with my fingers.

When the bowl was empty I used the cloth which had covered it to clean my hands, then replaced the bowl on the tray beside the cup which held Yan Quan's medicine. I refilled my own teacup and, after checking that my patient still slept, returned to my book. I had been reading about dreams, I remembered and I found the page again. That section of *The Physician's Vade Mecum* also contained information about something called *Remarkable Delusions* which looked interesting. I adjusted the lamp, drawing it closer, but it was still difficult to read. There was not enough light in here, not enough to read by, not enough to sit comfortably in this dark cabin. I would pull the curtains aside, just slightly, I decided.

It was not a big window and surely the light it would admit would not disturb the sick man. Pulling aside the cloth covering the glass, I moved my book so that the shaft of daylight which entered fell on the pages. Yes, that was better. I could see more clearly now, and Yan Quan had not stirred.

I flipped through the manual, searching for the description of *Remarkable Delusions*. Here is was, just after the part about dreams. Without taking my eyes from the book, I reached out for my tea and took a deep swallow, draining the cup.

Once more, I began to read.

Twelve

I t was hot, much too hot. Someone was calling me, calling
me loudly. That was most impolite because I didn't wish
to be disturbed. I would ignore the shouting.

"Wake up!"

I didn't want to wake up. I was tired, very tired. It seemed
to me that my head rested on a table and that a book served as
a pillow, but it didn't matter how uncomfortable my bed was.
I was asleep and I would not listen to that unmannerly voice.

"Wake up. There is danger."

Danger? That was ridiculous. I was only sleeping; what
could be dangerous in that? I wondered if maybe I should try
to raise my head and see what was wrong, but it was too
heavy to lift. I vaguely realized that I had drooled as I slept. I
wanted to wipe my face but I would have to wake up to do
that. I would sleep some more and then ...

"Master Percy, for your life. Wake up."

Master Percy? How cruel of J.B. to call me that. Or was it
my father who spoke to me?

"Master Percy, listen to me, listen well. There is danger,
great danger."

I knew that voice. Slowly, very slowly as if moving through layers of molasses, I raised my head.

"Wake up, Percy. Wake up and escape with your life!"

With difficulty I turned my head, peering into the corner of the Peace House from where the voice came. A tall man stood there, his face shadowed. I swallowed hard, suddenly afraid. He seemed to be wearing a thick necktie, but I could not see clearly. Why was the light so strange? A red glow came through the window, but it was not constant, flickering red, then orange, then dark again as if black clouds covered the sun.

No. Not clouds, I realized. Smoke. I could smell it. Thick smoke, billowing and blotting out for a moment the red glow of ...

"Fire! The town is burning and you will burn, too, if you do not wake up and run."

Wake up? But surely I was dreaming all of this: the voice, the smell of smoke, the red glow. I could not be awake. I *must* be having another nightmare. I must be dreaming. Only James Barry had ever called me Master Percy. He was dead, so if he were here in the room with me, I must be asleep. That was logical. That had to be true. Unless I were dead, too.

"Stand up, Master Percy. Stand!"

My head hurt and my legs felt too weak to hold me, but I knew that, dream or no dream, I had to obey. I leaned heavily on the table, pushing with my arms, forcing myself to stand. My legs buckled under me, and I fell back, groaning, knowing with a sick certainty that this was no dream. Nor was I dead. I was alive, awake and in danger.

"I can not stand," I said, the words pushing past my dry lips in a whisper. "I can not stand up."

It felt as if someone grabbed my arm and yanked me upright, for I was suddenly on my feet, standing unsteadily, but standing. Yet no one was near me. In the corner the tall man, who could not be who I knew he was, stood motionless in the red flickering light. Who, then, had lifted me?

"Run, Master Percy! To save your life, run from this place."

"Run?" Yes, that seemed a good idea. Slowly one foot moved ahead of the other but the floor heaved under me. "I can not run," I said.

"You must." Something seemed to give me a push from behind and my other foot moved. Again a push, then I took one last step and I was at the door. Both of my hands reached out and grasped the latch and then I thought of my patient.

"Yan Quan! I must help him."

The shadowed figure spoke urgently. "Leave him. He is in my care now. He will go with me."

"But ..."

"Time grows short, Ted. Run to save your life. To save my soul. Run!"

I pulled at the latch, but my fingers slipped from it. I reached out, grasped it again and pulled once more. The door slowly swung open and I stepped outside, into the street and into madness.

Smoke billowed about me, so thick that I could not see more than a few feet ahead. The noise of fire filled the air: the crackle of burning wood, the hiss of sparks landing on water, the crash of timbers falling to the ground. Shouts and screams echoed against the sound of running feet. Behind all the other noises, and louder than any of them, was the roar of the hungry flames.

There was a louder crash as a building collapsed. A gust of hot wind raced towards me, small glowing embers blown before it. I coughed as I drew a breath, then staggered as the movement sent a sharp pain through my head. I must run, but which way? Smoke surrounded me and, although I could not see the fire, I could hear it very near to me. I coughed again as another gust of wind blew down the street, clearing the smoke for a few seconds and showing more clearly the red flames licking up from the buildings ahead of me. I could not go in that direction, towards the main part of town. That way was barred by the fire which, even as I watched, took new life from the wind and blazed more fiercely, blocking the entire street with hot, hungry flames.

I must turn around, go up the road, go towards Richfield. The smoke hurt my throat and burned my lungs when I drew a breath. I coughed again. My head ached fiercely, throbbing with every movement I made. Surely I had fallen and injured my head, for it pained me so. I turned towards Richfield, taking one unsteady step, then another.

Why was it so hard to walk? Why did the ground seem to be made of cloth which shook and trembled under my feet? I must move away. I must run. He had said so.

Through the smoke ahead of me emerged a tall figure. "Ted? Ted?"

I stopped trying to move and stood so still that I did not even breathe. My heart raced as I peered through the haze, trying to see who called my name.

It could not be him, it could not be. I had left him in the cabin behind me. How could he be standing in front of me? He could *not* be here, he could not. "Go away," I said, taking a step backwards and nearly falling as I did so. "Leave me. Go away."

"Ted? Ted, is that you?" The figure moved nearer to me and I saw his face. It was J.B.

I remember him putting his arms around me and dragging me away from the fire. I remember how my head ached and how I could not move quickly and how J.B. kept urging me on, almost carrying me at times when the road became steep. I remember asking if my parents were safe, and I remember beginning to weep as I told J.B. I had left his new book in the Peace House and it would surely be destroyed.

I also remember saying, "He was there."

After that, I remember nothing.

"Where is he, Ted?"

"In the Peace House," I mumbled, through lips that were thick and dry. "In the corner, standing there."

"Standing? He was able to *stand*?"

Suddenly I came wide awake. I was in my own bed, still wearing my clothes, even my boots. My throat burned, my eyes stung and my vision was blurred. When I raised my hands to wipe my face, when I saw the soot on my palms and smelled the stale smoke on my hands, I remembered.

Fire! Barkerville was burning. I must escape! Sitting up, I swung my feet to the floor, ready to bolt from my bed and run to safety.

"Easy, Ted."

"J.B.? The fire. My parents ..."

"You are safe, your parents are too. They have gone to town to help those who have lost their homes. Your mother sat with you all night, but could not awaken you. I arrived after helping to fight the fire and she turned your care over to me." J.B. offered me water and I gulped it eagerly. He, too, smelled of smoke, but also of charred wood, singed hair and wet wool clothing. His eyebrows and eyelashes were gone and there was an ugly bruise across his forehead.

"Fire," I said. "I remember."

"Good. Then remember more. Where is he?"

I looked at J.B., not understanding. "I don't know," I said. "He was in the Peace House when I left."

"You *left* your patient? You abandoned Yan Quan?"

"Yan Quan? Is he safe?"

J.B. sighed. "That is exactly what I have been asking *you* for the past hour, Ted. Come to your senses. I have just returned from Barkerville, or what is left of it. The upper end, most of the Chinese section including the Peace House, was spared the worse of the fire although the rest of the town is nothing more than ashes."

"I'm glad," I said, relieved. "Then Yan Quan survived—or did his illness take him as you thought it would?"

"Ted, the Peace House is *empty*. I searched it thoroughly. Yan Quan's bed is unoccupied by either a live man or a corpse. He was too ill to move far on his own, but he has vanished. What happened to him?"

"He is gone? His bed is empty?"

J.B. sighed again, and offered me more water. "As empty as your head appears to be. Try to remember, Ted. You make no sense at all."

No sense at all, I thought. My head ached, and I found it hard to think. Nothing made sense, nothing.

"I don't remember. I don't understand. My head hurts. Did I injure it badly?"

"You injured it not at all, for I had a thorough look when I brought you home last night. However you kept complaining about it, also about the fact that the ground would not stay still beneath your feet. I realize that you were affected by the fumes you inhaled, but your symptoms and behaviour reminded me more of the time you took laudanum. That time, too, you slept until your parents despaired for you and awoke feeling sore-headed and irritable. Last night, when we cleared the soot from you face, I saw that you were also covered with a red rash, something I feel sure was not caused by the fire. What happened to you?"

"I don't know."

"Sing Kee told me that he left a vial of opium for you to give to Yan Quan. Are you sure you did not take some of it?"

Indignantly, I shook my head, then wished that I had kept it still. "I took no medication at all ... opium?" Of course, that was what was in the slender glass bottle. That was why the smell had seemed familiar when I added it to the tea.

The tea! I drank the remainder of Yan Quan's tea, thinking it was mine. The second cup had tasted more bitter than the first, I remembered, but I had been reading and had not paid much attention.

"I did take the drug," I said, "by mistake. I drank from the wrong cup." No wonder the ground had seemed to move beneath my feet as J.B. had helped me away from the fire. No wonder my legs were unsteady and my head hurt.

"That would explain much, but it still does not explain the fact that you have lost a patient. Now, if your head is clear, tell me what happened yesterday. Tell me everything."

For a long moment, I did not speak. Then, softly, I said, "I can not. For I am not sure myself."

"Try," said the doctor. He looked at me strangely. "Surely you did not carry Yan Quan away from the Peace House. You were in no shape to do that as I well know, for it was I who had to carry you."

"Thank you, J.B. I remember that."

"Then try to remember more."

Avoiding his eyes, I answered reluctantly. "I can not tell you any more. I do not know what happened in the Peace House. I do not know where Yan Quan is. I know nothing."

J.B. stood up and took several paces around the room. He spoke aloud, musing to himself as I had often heard him do when he was considering what to do about a patient.

"The lad remembers nothing, or so he says. But somehow he awoke from a drugged sleep—and we must remember that he has a particular sensitivity to that drug and would not have returned to consciousness easily. It was a miracle he awoke at all, but this wakening saved his life. The fumes from the smoke would have surely killed him had he remained where he was. Once awake, he had enough presence of mind to leave the cabin and attempt to escape the fire, although he could barely hold himself upright. Now, although his memory has returned, he resists revealing the rest of the story."

I stared at the floor and was silent. J.B. took another turn around my bedroom, still speaking as if to himself. "Does he tell the truth? He is an honest lad, not given to falsehoods, yet he claims to know nothing more. This is a particularly perplexing problem which prompts me to ..."

"Stop that!"

"Ah. The patient's temper has survived his ordeal. I consider that a sign of imminent recovery."

He stopped pacing and returned to my bedside, sitting down and waiting until I lifted my head and looked at him. "The disappearance of Yan Quan is not so terrible, Ted, although I despair of your success as a physician if you continue to lose patients in this mysterious way. The man was dying; he may have been dead when you left. It is possible that his countrymen removed his body. I will ask Sing Kee and perhaps he can tell us what happened."

"I think not," I said doubtfully, remembering the voice from the shadows telling me that Yan Quan was in "his" care and would go with him.

"Ted, what is wrong? You have turned pale and look near to fainting."

I kept silent. What could I say? How could I tell J.B. that I believed that my patient had been taken by someone or something who did not exist?

"Ted, you have been far away. Please return to the present."

I blinked and found, to my surprise, that my eyes were damp. "I am here, J.B."

Again he looked at me strangely. "Perhaps one day you will tell me more. But now, I must go. There is much to be done in Barkerville—many burns, scrapes, and coughs to attend to. Although I have no dispensary and nothing to dispense, no supplies, no bed, no ..."

"J.B.! Your surgery burned down?"

"It did. Everything is gone. All my books—except this one, which you so kindly left on the table in the Peace House." Smiling, he held up *The Physician's Vade Mecum*. "This book and my small black bag, which I had the foresight to grab when I ran from the approaching flames, now represent my entire surgery, dispensary, and reference library."

"It's all gone? Everything?"

"Everything. So, once I have done what I can do for the distraught inhabitants of Barkerville, I will leave."

"Leave? What will you do?"

"I will become a travelling physician, wandering around the goldfields with my invaluable reference book, trusting nature and luck to provide for me, offering my services where I can."

"I could come with you."

"Ted, Barkerville now has a much greater need of carpenters than of physicians. If you listen carefully you can hear, drifting up the hill, the sounds of great activity. The ashes of the town are scarcely cool but already people have begun rebuilding what was lost. Your father has made plans for you. His shop was damaged but still stands, and customers are lining up outside his charred door begging him to work for them. He is in great need of a capable assistant."

"I don't want to ..."

"Your father needs your help, Ted. Barkerville needs your carpentry skills. I, however, do not need an assistant at the moment, having no place where you can assist and nothing for you to assist me with. I think your course of action should be clear."

"But ..."

J.B. stood, pushing back the chair on which he had been sitting. "I must leave, Ted. Regain your strength quickly. Your help is greatly needed."

Carefully, I swung my feet onto the floor and stood up. My head still hurt slightly, but my legs were strong again and my mind was clear. This was no time to be lounging about in bed. There was work to do.

J.B. picked up his doctor's bag and began to walk towards the door, but then he turned to me once more.

"I know you do not wish to speak of what occurred yesterday, Ted, but there is something which puzzles me. You said, one of the few sensible things I managed to hear as I dragged your uncooperative person away, you said, '*He* was there.'"

"Did I?"

"Indeed you did, as I suspect you know full well."

"It was nothing," I said. "A dream."

How could I tell J.B. that a ghost had stolen a sick man, that a murderer had returned from the grave to offer me help? These things did not happen. There were no ghosts and I did not believe in them anyway. Maybe I *had* dreamt it, or maybe it was the effects of the drugged tea or maybe ...

I remembered what he had said, the 'he' who could not have been there. "Run, Master Percy, to save your life." And then, the last words he spoke, "To save my soul."

"I do not think it was a dream," said J.B. "Who was there, Ted? Who was with you?"

"I do not know," I answered, and that was the truth.

HISTORICAL NOTES

The events in this story take place in Barkerville between April and September 1868.

MAIN CHARACTERS

Ted

Theodore Percival MacIntosh, better known as Ted, is fictional. He appears first in *Moses, Me and Murder* (Pacific Educational Press), where the story of the murder of Charles Blessing and the subsequent arrest, trial, and hanging of James Barry is fully told. The third book in the series, *By the Skin of His Teeth* (The Dundurn Group), takes up where *The Doctor's Apprentice*, the second book, leaves off.

Doctor J.B. Wilkinson

J.B. (whose middle name I never did learn) practised medicine in Barkerville for many years and is buried in the cemetery there. His story and his relationship with Sophia Cameron is much as I have told it in this book. Nowhere did I find any historical evidence that he abused drugs; however, since opium was as widely used in the nineteenth century as aspirin is today, I invented a drug dependency for him. Because of his role as Sophia Cameron's physician and because he was one of the men who helped Cariboo Cameron carry her body away from the goldfields, I did not believe it would be a great leap of faith to assume that Doctor Wilkinson would have suffered some form of depression or other mental anguish as a result of those experiences. He was only thirty-five years old when he died on November 3, 1869.

Washington (or Wellington) Delaney Moses
Moses was a barber in Barkerville for many years, and his shop is a major display in the restored town. His role in the Blessing/Barry affair is well documented as he was the principal witness against James Barry.

Mr. Malanion
Mr. Malanion (probably a misspelling of the French "Malamon") was a violin player who had been a member of the Paris Opera Orchestra. Malanion spent many years in Barkerville giving music lessons. His grave is also in the Barkerville Cemetery.

Sing Kee
There were many Chinese who came to the goldfields, and most towns had an herbalist like Sing Kee. Much of what he sold was imported from China, but he may have grown some of his own herbs on terraced gardens on the hillsides of Barkerville. Sing Kee no doubt sold opium from his shop, for the Chinese were among the first to realize the great benefits the drug offered. Opium, in a solid form, was also smoked by some members of the Chinese community. Sing Kee's store and samples of his wares are on display in Barkerville.

James Barry
James Barry was tried in front of Judge Begbie ("The Hanging Judge") and was found guilty of the murder of Charles Blessing.

He was hanged on August 8, 1867, but whether his ghost ever walked the streets of Barkerville, I do not know.

Other Characters
Like Ted, his parents are fictitious, as are Mrs. Fraser, the twins, and Bridget. All other characters mentioned by name are real people, including the doctors to whose research J.B. sometimes refers.

PLACES, THINGS, AND EVENTS

The Peace House (Tai Ping Fong)
The Peace House, also called the Peace Room or Tai Ping Fong, was a haven for indigent Chinese who were too ill to care for themselves. Others brought them food and cared for them; many men died in that tiny cabin or one much like it. It was customary to unearth the bodies several years after death and send the bones back to China to be reburied. A replica of the Peace House stands behind the Tong building in today's Barkerville.

The Physician's Vade Mecum
In 1823 Doctor Hooper of London published the first *Vade Mecum*, stating in his preface that he intended to provide a "concise treatise on the practice of medicine for the use of Student and Practitioner." The book was so successful that it was reprinted many times with new sections added as medical knowledge increased. The 1868 edition, updated and revised by Doctors William A. Guy and John Harley, is the one I used for reference. It contains almost everything a physician of

that time needed to know—how to treat milk fever; how to ease pain; how to recognize diphtheria, meningitis, or measles; how to prepare salves or purgatives; and even how to amputate limbs. It was an invaluable source of information about the practice of medicine at the time of the events of this book.

The Barkerville Fire

On September 16, 1868, at a quarter to three in the afternoon, a fire started in Barkerville in a building near Barry and Adler's Saloon. The most commonly believed story is that a miner was trying to steal a kiss from a saloon girl who was ironing, and he knocked against the stovepipe of the wood stove on which she was heating her flatiron. By four-thirty, the whole town, with the exception of a few buildings in the upper section, was on fire. By ten o'clock the next morning, reconstruction had already begun and continued at a great pace until the town was rebuilt, much as it can be seen today. Since no one died or vanished in the Barkerville Fire, Yan Quan is my own invention. What really happened to him remains a mystery, even to me.

ANN WALSH is the author of *Flower Power, Your Time, My Time, Shabash!* (nominated for the Silver Birch Award), and *The Ghost of Soda Creek* (a Canadian Library Association's Notable Selection). She is also the creator of the Barkerville historical mystery series, whose novels include *Moses, Me and Murder, The Doctor's Apprentice,* and *By the Skin of His Teeth.* As an editor, she has published three anthologies of children's stories, *Winds Through Time, Beginnings,* and *Dark Times.* All her books have received the Canadian Children's Book Centre Our Choice Award. She lives in Williams Lake, British Columbia.